The Windmill Café

Christmas Trees

Poppy Blake is an avid scribbler of contemporary romance and romcoms. When not writing she loves indulging in the odd cocktail or two – accompanied by a tower of cupcakes. The Windmill Café series follows the life and loves of Rosie and Matt in the glorious countryside of Norfolk. Why not pop in for a visit?

@poppyblakebooks

www.facebook.com/poppy.blake.395

Also in this series

The Windmill Café – Summer Breeze
The Windmill Café – Autumn Leaves

The Windmill Café

Christmas Trees

Poppy Blake

A division of HarperCollins*Publishers*
www.harpercollins.co.uk

Harper*Impulse* an imprint of
HarperCollins*Publishers*
The News Building
1 London Bridge Street
London SE1 9GF

www.harpercollins.co.uk

This paperback edition 2018

First published in Great Britain in ebook format by
HarperCollins*Publishers* 2018

A catalogue record for this book
is available from the British Library

ISBN: 978-0-00-832538-1

This novel is entirely a work of fiction.
The names, characters and incidents portrayed in it are
the work of the author's imagination. Any resemblance to
actual persons, living or dead, events or localities is
entirely coincidental.

Set in Birka by Palimpsest Book Production Limited,
Falkirk, Stirlingshire

Printed and bound in Great Britain
by CPI Group (UK) Ltd, Croydon CR0 4YY

To Mum and Dad; I know you would be so proud to see
my name on the cover of a novel

Chapter 1

Rosie trotted down the spiral staircase from her studio above the Windmill Café with a song in her heart and a spring in her step. When she reached the bottom step, the smile melted from her lips and the clutter demons began to circle, causing the muscles in her stomach to contract and a familiar light-headedness threaten to overwhelm her.

'Oh my God, Mia! What's going on?'

'Hi, Rosie. I thought I'd make a start on choosing the design for our entry into the Christmas Tree Carousel competition on Saturday. Which theme do you think we should go for? Gastronomic Gorgeousness with these cute knitted cupcakes? Or what about Windmill Wonderfulness with these little wooden windmill-shaped decorations?'

'Neither! We're hosting the contest – not taking part!'

'The two are not mutually exclusive! We're not involved in the judging, that's the Rev's unenviable task, so why shouldn't we be allowed to join in the fun?' Mia held up a cherubic ornament that had seen better days, a smile stretching her lips. 'Don't you think this angel is simply adorable? Hey, we could go with a celestial theme – you know, fluffy white clouds made of cotton wool and glitter, home-made silver stars, papier-mâché moons, a few planets and these sweet little angels?'

'Mia—'

'What? You prefer something along the lines of my first suggestions? A creative culinary masterpiece? Actually, I do love those miniature silver whisks and spatulas you sourced for the Christmas crackers, and we could use the doll's house kitchenware Grace found in the vicarage's attic instead of baubles.'

Rosie heaved a sigh at her friend's bubbling enthusiasm. However, there was no way she could stay irritated with Mia for long as she watched her skip from one decrepit cardboard box to the next, dipping her hands into the treasure inside like a toddler taking part in her first Christmas lucky dip. Like her approach to Christmas tree decorating, Mia had a quirky dress sense too – more nineteen sixties flower-power than twenty-first century chic. That day's outfit was a pair of white dungarees embroidered with what might have looked to a casual onlooker like silver snowflakes, but were in fact bunches of cutlery.

Rosie allowed herself a wry smile – at least Mia had ditched the sausage-bedecked apron that usually forced their customers to perform a double-take just to make sure it wasn't depicting something altogether more risqué. She loved Mia and was grateful for the way she had welcomed her into the community of Willerby with an all-encompassing hug, not to mention introducing her to the group of people she was now lucky enough to call friends. What she struggled with was the chaos that Mia scattered in her fragrant wake; and if there was one thing Rosie didn't cope with very well it was clutter.

The tickle of alarm she'd experienced when she'd walked into the café was now threatening to burgeon into full-blown panic. Her heartrate increased even further when her eyes landed on the twisted garlands of lurid pink tinsel, the mounds of multi-coloured paperchains, and the tumble of old-fashioned glass baubles that were piled high on every available surface as well as the floor. Prickles of perspiration swept uncomfortably across her skin. She commenced the counting exercises her sister Georgina had taught her for when such occasions threatened to overwhelm her, but that morning those techniques did not help to wash away the mounting stress. Diversionary tactics were called for.

'I thought I'd rustle up a few dozen mince pies, and maybe a batch of chocolate yule logs and some iced ginger biscuits for the party after the judging on Saturday. What do you think?'

'Great idea. If you give me a few minutes, I'll help—'

'No! You just concentrate on repacking all this—stuff—into the right boxes and taking it back to your car.'

Mia paused in her contemplation of an overweight plastic gnome dressed in a Santa suit, her green eyes creasing in apology. 'Sorry, Rosie. I forgot about your aversion to—well, to all this…' She swept her hand around the room, lifting her mahogany waves from her face and dropping them over her shoulder in a familiar gesture. 'I truly only intended to bring one box of ornaments over, but I just got carried away. Let's go with the culinary theme, eh?'

'Agreed!'

Rosie exhaled a long calming breath, blew a wayward cooper curl from her lashes and began to help Mia return as much of the festive paraphernalia as possible to its cardboard home. When they had finished she waited for Mia to balance the boxes in a wobbly stack and carry them to the car park before selecting one of the Windmill Café's peppermint-and-white aprons and turning her attention to the mince pies. Baking had always provided her with a sojourn of solace when all those around her were going crazy, and she couldn't wait to delve her hands into a bowl of flour to get her fix.

But she couldn't blame Mia for her enthusiasm. What had she expected? It was the week before Christmas, this sort of frenzied behaviour always happened at that time of year. For the first time, she was spending Christmas in the close-knit community of Willerby, the Norfolk village whose residents had woven their personal brand of magic through her veins. She loved it here and that was one of the reasons she had agreed to host the inaugural Christmas tree decorating competition at the café – to say a heartfelt thank you to everyone for their kindness. It was just that she hadn't expected so many entries! Fourteen!

For a woman who loved to be organised and in control of every aspect of her life, Rosie definitely hadn't thought through her seasonal gesture properly. She was fully aware of the cause of that unfortunate lapse in concentration – as was Mia – and for that she was paying the price. However, she refused to linger on the grenade-splattered landscape of her love life and began to rub the shards of cold butter into the flour to make the shortcrust pastry. Immediately, the tension in the back of her neck started to dissipate and when she added the orange and lemon zest, her mood improved even further and she could envisage the arrangements for Saturday's competition begin to slot into the schedule template etched on her brain.

'I'll make us some coffee,' said Mia when she returned, pressing their prized Gaggia machine into action. 'Freddie called when I was at the car. He's on his way over to set up the marquee this afternoon, and then he and Matt will deliver the trees tomorrow – no cost because they sourced them from the woodland around Ultimate Adventures. That'll please Graham!'

Rosie rolled her eyes at the mention of the habitually absent owner of the Windmill Café – and the adjacent luxury holiday site that housed a selection of Scandinavian lodges and a perfectly proportioned shepherd's hut painted in the same colours as the windmill and its sails. Once again, with a regularity that was becoming highly suspicious, Graham had managed to come up with an unbreakable prior engagement – this time with a snowboard in the Swiss Alps – when she and Mia had presented their plans for the café's Christmas promotional event. At the Summer Breeze garden party in August, her erstwhile boss had taken a 'well-earned' break from the routine in his villa in Barbados, and during the Autumn Leaves bash he had sailed away from Palma harbour on his brother's yacht.

However, his absence had turned out to be fortuitous because on each occasion one of the guests staying in the holiday lodges had suffered a terrible accident. First, pop star-to-be Suki Richards had been poisoned, and then Rick Forster, an avid myth-seeker, had been shot with a bow and arrow. Fortunately, both incidents had been wrapped up by the time Graham returned home and he'd only heard the details after the event – a much better scenario as far as Rosie was concerned. In fact, had Graham been there she suspected he would never have agreed to their plans to hold the Christmas Tree Carousel competition at the Windmill Café and Mia would have been devastated. Nevertheless, this time she had every intention of ensuring that everything ran smoothly.

'Do you think we're crazy?' asked Rosie as she slid the last batch of mince pies into the oven and began the ritual of squirting every worktop with anti-bacterial spray to eradicate any lingering germ from existence. Whilst she loved the delicious aroma of nutmeg, cinnamon and cloves that was currently ballooning through the air, she preferred the satisfying smell of Flash with a top note of chlorine.

'What do you mean?'

'Holding the competition the day before Grace and Josh's wedding?'

'It's perfect!' declared Mia, as usual only seeing the positive in any given situation. 'It means that their guests can take part in the contest too. It's a great way to break the ice and give everyone something else to focus on before the frenzy starts.'

'And added another six people to our competitors list!'

'The more the merrier! We'll set up the trees in the marquee tomorrow morning, and then, after the men's cycle race has finished, the contestants can make a start. That'll give everyone a full three days to complete their masterpieces before the judging takes place on Saturday afternoon.'

Rosie finished her session of extreme cleaning with a flourish and felt the last vestiges of her earlier stress drain from her veins. She swept her eyes around the room, satisfied it was as pristine as she had left it the previous evening before Mia had landed with her cornucopia of Christmas knick-knacks.

'It's a bit of an usual activity for a stag party, don't you think? A ten-mile cycle race?' said Rosie, wrinkling her nose in bewilderment at Josh's choice of pre-wedding celebration with his closest friends.

'Not if cycling is your passion. And according to Grace, Josh is not only passionate about his bike, he's obsessed! You know, last weekend he did the Coast-to-Coast with his best man, Sam, and a group of other friends who couldn't make it down to Norfolk this week. If I were Grace I'd have him on flower arranging duties!'

'So how many are taking part in the stag party sprint in the morning?'

'Well, according to Freddie, apart from Josh and Sam, there'll be another three; Dylan, Abbi's boyfriend, Theo, an old friend of Josh's who's arranged the wedding cars at mate's rates, and Archie, everyone's favourite pub landlord from the Drunken Duck; so seven guys in total, if you include Matt and Freddie.

At the mention of Matt's name, Rosie averted her eyes from Mia's and became interested in choosing the perfect mince pie to go with her coffee, the surge of warmth spreading across her cheeks having nothing to do with the heat from the oven and everything to do with Mia's not-so-casual reference to the owner of Ultimate Adventures.

'You've got to talk to Matt, Rosie.'

'I have talked to Matt!'

'You know what I mean – about Harry's proposition.'

'I haven't decided what to do yet.'

'Even more reason why the two of you should have a chat. Okay, so we all know you turned down Harry's marriage proposal – we were there when he dropped the bombshell on you at the Autumn Leaves party. And, if I might add, you made the right decision when you chose to go with your gut instinct.'

Rosie's lips twitched in amusement at her friend's candour. 'Thank you, Mia, I'm pleased you—'

'What I'm talking about is Harry's business proposition. I don't blame you for *thinking* about it, it was a great offer – a half share of a florist business in Pimlico is not to be tossed away without very careful consideration, especially when you were so good at it before Harry messed up by frolicking amongst the blooms with a random selection of blushing brides.'

'Hardly a random selection, there was only Heidi...'

'As far as you know,' added Mia, impishly. 'But even as his *business* partner, I ask you one question, Rosie. Can you trust him? Are his motives selfless? Or has he simply discovered the hard way that it was *your* creative talent that attracted all those lucrative bridal contracts, not his, and he regrets letting you go?'

'That's three questions!'

'And here's another two. How can you even contemplate leaving the Windmill Café? And won't you miss Matt?'

'Mia, I've told you, I love it here, but I'm just the part-time manager of a small holiday site that practically runs itself, and a café that is currently only open on Saturdays and Sundays until Easter. If, and it's only an if, if I accept Harry's proposition I will be the legal owner of a successful business enterprise in London. Before I stumbled on Harry and Heidi amongst the roses, I had a kaleidoscope of fresh ideas to take wedding floristry to new heights, you know that.'

'Well, I don't know how you can even contemplate working alongside that unfaithful, disloyal, lying moron!' huffed Mia, who had spent the remainder of the Autumn Leaves party after Harry's shock appearance – and very public marriage and business proposal – glaring at him as though he was the Big Bad Wolf personified. Even after he had left, having spent a fruitless weekend trying to persuade Rosie that he was truly sorry for what he had done, assuring her that Heidi was ancient history and that he'd learned his lesson and would never repeat it, Mia had refused to speak about him, apart from labelling him a Dastardly Destroyer of Dreams. 'Anyway, Matt misses you.'

'Matt has avoided me for six weeks.'

Rosie experienced the familiar mule's kick to the stomach when she uttered those pain-filled words. In the months leading up to Harry's arrival at the end of October, she had grown close to Matt Wilson, the hunky owner of the outward-bound activity centre hidden in the woodland on the other side of Willerby, through their amateur sleuthing activities. More than that, Grace had even invited them both to her wedding on Christmas Eve and Rosie had been delighted to accept, especially as Mia's meddling had meant she was going as Matt's Plus One – until Harry had popped up unannounced and thrown a spanner in the works.

'You and Matt are made for each other!' declared Mia,

grabbing a mince pie from the wire cooling rack and slumping down onto one of the café's white leather sofas, holding her palm under her chin to catch any wayward crumbs – a crime punishable by a ferocious glare from Rosie.

'Mia, I'm still friends with Matt. It's his decision to avoid me and the café.'

But Rosie knew Mia wasn't listening to her assurances because she was intent on delivering her own agenda.

'You and Matt make a fabulous team. You solved those crimes before the police had even finished slurping their coffee! When you're together, you are greater than the sum of your parts – and not just in the puzzle-wrangling arena. There's something almost effervescent about you when he's by your side – something that's completely missing when Harry's around. I watched you carefully when Harry graced us with his presence again at the beginning of December to press his case. Your sparkle was missing-in-action – he snuffs it out with his overbearing personality.'

Mia flicked her fingers to emphasise her point.

'Do you really want to go back to being the old Rosie? Okay, so you were a florist to the stars and that's amazing, but what you have here is more than just a job. You have a *home* and you are surrounded by friends who love you – not to mention a guy who thinks the world of you. When Matt, and Freddie, offer their help, they want nothing in return – unlike Harry!'

Rosie couldn't fault Mia for her impassioned submissions on behalf of Matt. Everything she had said was true. Matt had come to her aid when she had been accused of poisoning one of the lodge guests with her baking, and she had returned the favour when one of his outward-bound clients had been speared with an arrow, an incident that had threatened the future of his business. There had been no expectations of anything in return, simply a celebratory drink at the local pub, the Drunken Duck.

'It isn't that Matt's not speaking to you, Rosie. He's a decent guy, and he just wants to give you the space to make your decision without any external influences. He's wrong on this occasion, in my opinion. He should be standing right here in front of you, telling you exactly why you should tell Harry to get lost and to stay where you are cherished – if not for your cheerful and generous personality, then certainly for your fig-and-walnut scones and these fabulous St. Clements mince pies.'

Mia did have a point. Harry's reappearance in her life had sent Matt away. Once she had persuaded her ex-boyfriend that her response to his marriage proposal was a resounding *no!* she had promised to think about his business proposition, arguing to herself that she would be crazy not to.

When Harry made the return trip to Willerby at the beginning of December, he had brought with him the accounts, as well as a formal legal contract setting everything out in black-and-white that she would be a part-owner of the florist's shop and business. Harry had been stoical about her rejection of marriage, but urged her not to turn down the chance of financial security for the rest of her life – unlike her position as the Windmill Café manager which, if the last few months were anything to go by, was precarious in the extreme.

However, what had really caused her to prevaricate over Harry's offer was the fact that if she lost her job at the café, she would also lose her home and she didn't think she could go through that trauma again. Residing in the dark recesses of her mind was a hard nugget of fear that history would repeat itself, and her dreams were filled with memories of the day her mother had been forcibly evicted from the family home after her father's death. The incident had changed the path of her life and had been the catalyst for her battle with the cleanliness demons. She had no idea how she was going to make the decision, though, and Harry's increasingly regular phone calls were not helping.

She had tried to seek Matt out, to reassure him that their friendship was unaffected by the recent turn of events. However, when she had arrived on the doorstep of the wooden reception cabin at Ultimate Adventures, Freddie had explained to her that Matt had jumped on a last-minute flight to Tenerife to climb Mount Teide with a group of his father's climbing buddies, and since his return two weeks ago he had steadfastly avoided her.

'Maybe there'll be another mystery for you to solve that will bring you back together,' mused Mia as she drained the dregs of her coffee and went to wash her mug in the sink and return it to its allotted space.

'God, I hope not! All our lodge guests are here for the stag party and then to celebrate the wedding on Sunday. Grace, not to mention, the Rev and Carole, would be mortified if anything untoward happened to them!'

Chapter 2

'Oh my God! It's freezing! I can't believe the guys still wanted to take part in the cycle race instead of adjourning to the pub for a cosy few pints like most stag party enthusiasts!' said Rosie, screwing up her nose in disgust as she wrapped her arms around her waist in an effort to fend off the relentless downpour and keep warm. 'More to the point, I can't believe you managed to persuade me to form part of the welcoming committee!'

A shiver of discomfort shot down her spine as she peered through the gloom into the densely packed woodland at the rear of the outward-bound centre. Ultimate Adventures offered a plethora of activities including mountaineering, gorge scrambling, a treetop zip wire adventure, and even an obstacle course that mixed physical strength with mental agility. She could understand how these pursuits would be appealing in the summer months, but not on a wet Wednesday morning in the middle of December. In fact, there was something almost menacing about the way the naked trees crowded forward, blocking out what little light was left in the pewter-coloured sky.

'Lots of cycle addicts love this kind of weather – makes the whole ride much more interesting.' Mia laughed as she blew on her palms and clapped her mittened hands together in excitement. 'Anyway, it's just a shower.'

'This isn't a shower, it's a monsoon!'

The rain was coming down in stair rods, hammering the wooden planks of the reception's veranda with a vicious acrimony and drenching the small but courageous – and some might say crazy – gathering of spectators at the finish line. Rosie tightened the hood of her padded jacket around her chin in an attempt to prevent her curls from ballooning like copper candyfloss but she was fighting a losing battle.

'And you never know, maybe this rain will turn into snow,' beamed Grace, the end of her perfectly-formed nose tinged pink from the cold. 'Don't you think that would make an absolutely amazing backdrop for our wedding photographs?'

'And the Christmas tree competition!' added Mia with a glint of mischief in her eyes as she glanced across at Rosie.

'I agree with Rosie,' mumbled Abbi, Grace's best friend and chief bridesmaid, as she twirled her frilly cerise umbrella over her shoulder like a female version of Gene Kelly and frowned up at the bruised sky.

Rosie experienced a stab of empathy when she saw that Abbi's previously smooth bob was no longer straight but plastered haphazardly to her cheeks and forehead. The pale pink sequinned stilettos that matched the gorgeous leather satchel she had designed and hand-sewn herself were clearly no match against the onslaught of rain gods.

'Give me a tropical beach anytime!' Abbi continued. 'If

Dylan ever gets around to proposing to me, I'm definitely opting for wall-to-wall sunshine, a pretty white gazebo on the sand and as many palm trees swaying in the breeze as possible.'

'Well, I could hardly do that, could I? Mum and Dad would have killed me if I'd decided to get married anywhere other than at St Andrews!' giggled Grace, as she flicked her messy blond curls behind her ears and squinted into the distance for a potential early glimpse of the cyclists. 'Anyway, I happen to think every season has its own splendour.'

'Oh, me too,' declared Penny, Theo's girlfriend who, like Grace, had been keen to be part of the boys' intrepid welcoming committee. 'I love all the raw, tempestuous beauty of the natural environment. There's almost a mystical aura hanging over the foliage, don't you think? I can easily imagine this whole place being populated by a horde of mythical beasts; the ivy-laced boughs their playground, the hidden copses where they take an afternoon snooze. It's the perfect inspiration for my next children's book. I can't wait to get my pencils out when I get back to the lodge and start sketching.'

As if to prove her artistic credentials, she pulled out her mobile phone and took a few random photographs of the surrounding woodland, sending a whiff of patchouli oil into the air and causing the plethora of silver chains to jangle against her ample chest. With her penchant for wearing black, from her heavily drawn makeup down to the colour of her nail polish, she occupied the opposite end of the sartorial colour spectrum to Abbi.

Rosie recalled booking Penny and Theo into their luxury Scandinavian lodge the previous day and had been amazed at the amount of painting equipment Penny had brought with her. Canvases of varying sizes, paint palettes, a whole battalion of brushes. There was so much stuff that a casual observer could have been forgiven for thinking she was running an artist's retreat for the other guests at the Windmill lodges, which included Josh's best man and his wife, Sam and Zara, as well as Abbi and Dylan – who had turned down the luxury lodge to stay in the cute peppermint-and-white shepherd's hut despite its size. When she had suggested one of the larger lodges, Abbi had reminded her that after spending the summer backpacking in south east Asia, the shepherd's hut was the height of decadence for them.

'Hey, Penny, do you think you could do a pastel sketch of St Andrew's church as a wedding present for us?'

'Wow, yes, I'd love to!'

'Oh, do you do portraits? I'd love one of the twins,' said Zara, tucking her neat mahogany curls behind her ears, her face brightening when she spoke of her two boys currently having the time of their lives at their grandparents' farm in the Lake District.

'No problem,' smiled Penny, clearly delighted to have got two commissions in the space of five minutes.

Rosie cast her eyes around the group of women from beneath her lashes. Despite the inclement weather, everyone had managed to achieve a sense of style. Compared to them, she felt like Cinderella's bedraggled cousin in the mismatched outfit she had selected that morning for comfort and practicality rather than sartorial elegance. Why hadn't *she* worn a jaunty bright orange hat-scarf-and-gloves combo like Zara, or a quirky leather jacket like Penny? Of course, Mia had chosen a white down-filled jacket she had embellished herself with appliqué snowflakes and what Rosie had assumed were branches adorned with red berries but had turned out to be reindeer antlers and Rudolph noses.

When her eyes fell towards her footwear, Rosie cringed. Olive-green Wellington boots weren't the most glamorous of attire – although they did match her wax jacket. She really should have made more of an effort, especially as this was the first time she would be seeing Matt in weeks. However, she reminded herself that Matt wasn't the kind of person who judged a book by its glossy cover and she relaxed.

'Look! Here they come!' cried Mia, shielding her eyes with her hand and pointing towards a flicker of luminous yellow Lycra just beyond the row of conifers standing to attention like a battalion of sentries guarding the road that lead to the reception lodge. 'Can you see who's out in front? Is it Matt or Freddie? Oh, I really hope it's Freddie!'

'It won't be if Theo has anything to do with it!' muttered Penny with a roll of her kohl-rimmed eyes and a twist of her upper lip. 'You've no idea how competitive he is. He'd even try to outride Chris Hoy!'

'Well, it definitely won't be Dylan,' laughed Abbi. 'He's more of a Sunday afternoon cyclist – with plenty of planned beer stops at as many rural pubs as he can get away with. He hates all this racing malarkey. However, you should have seen the look on his face when he saw the zip wire earlier – he almost swooned! I suspect he might be tempted to renege on his promise to enter your Christmas tree decorating contest, Rosie, in favour of spending some time flying through the air like Peter Pan's older brother.'

Abbi had mentioned Dylan's aversion to anything conducted at high speed, especially whilst on two wheels, on a couple of occasions and Rosie wondered what had happened to cause that but didn't like to pry. She couldn't wait to welcome all seven men back safely so they could return to the café and make a start on the best part of the day – sipping mugs of creamy hot chocolate laced with a generous dash of brandy and sampling the mini cappuccino roulades she had whipped up earlier, before everyone was let loose on their respective Christmas trees.

'Yay! You were both wrong!' squealed Grace, pogoing up and down on the spot, clapping her hands in jubilation. 'It's Josh! Come on, Josh! Come on, Josh!'

Rosie watched as the frontrunner finally emerged from the arboreal sanctuary and raced down the main driveway towards the veranda where Theo had insisted that they rigged up a makeshift red ribbon for the winner to drive through. Grace was right, her husband-to-be *was* in the lead, but only by a few seconds as Freddie had appeared from another gap in the trees ten metres to Josh's left, his head bent low over the handlebars, pumping his legs with dogged determination. Her heart gave a pleasurable nip when she saw that Matt was in third place. It was all she could do to prevent herself from cupping her hands around her lips and screaming *Go Matt!* in a very unladylike fashion until Mia linked arms with her and Grace.

'Come on, ladies. Let's get over to the finishing line. You

too, Penny – we might need a photo-finish! Coming Zara? Abbi?'

Rosie watched Abbi stand on her tiptoes to scan the fringe of the woodland for any sign of Dylan, anxiety creasing her forehead as she chewed on her lower lip. It was a few nerve-wracking minutes before she spotted him fifty metres of so behind Sam.

'Oh, thank God! There's Dylan – bringing up the rear as usual!' Abbi sighed, but Rosie saw the relief spread across her attractive features. She might bemoan her boyfriend's lack of expertise when it came to vehicular activities but she clearly worried about him all the same. 'I thought he might have fallen off or something.'

Everyone rushed through the drizzle to where Penny had crouched down onto her haunches next to a wooden post and levelled her mobile phone camera, poised to snap a picture of the victor's triumphant achievement.

'Yay! Yay! Josh!' screeched Grace, rushing forward to embrace her fiancé before reaching up to kiss him tenderly on the lips. Her evident excitement lit up her pretty face, framed by a ruffle of damp corkscrew curls that sprang from beneath her woolly bobble hat.

Freddie was next over the finishing line, a wide grin splitting his freckled face as he yanked off his safety helmet and strode over to offer Josh a congratulatory handshake.

'Great ride, Josh, especially the last hundred metres!'

'You too, mate. That was awesome. I might even be forced to rethink my earlier criticism of Theo's insistence that we start the stag celebrations with a gruelling cross-country race! Now

I can't wait to have a go at the Ultimate Adventure's obstacle course and the zip wire. Although don't tell him I said that. He has a habit of letting compliments go to his head!'

Matt skidded to a halt next, his whole body covered in random speckles of flying mud, even his cheeks, followed by Sam. Rosie's stomach gave an uncomfortable twist when she saw that Matt was looking directly at her. However, before she could say anything to him, Abbi had shoved her to one side to welcome Dylan like a conquering hero.

'Yay! Dylan! You did it!'

Dylan removed his helmet and ran his fingers through his spiky ebony hair, his face a curious shade of overworked putty, his jaw clenched tight after being forced to endure his personal idea of purgatory. His relief the ride was at an end was palpable.

'Never, ever, *ever* ask me to do that again!' Dylan spluttered, his breath coming in ragged spurts as he struggled to regain his composure. 'Why couldn't we have gone for a few drinks at the local pub like any normal stag party? Theo Morris has to be one of the hardest task-masters I've ever come across and that includes the physio guys at the hospital!'

'Speaking of Theo, where is he?' asked Rosie, looking back down the winding, leaf-strewn roadway towards the stone pillars that guarded the entrance gate to Ultimate Adventures. Everyone paused in what they were doing to squint through the gloom of the trees but there was no sign of the director in charge of Dylan's horror movie.

'Actually, I have to admit that I thought it was strange he wasn't in pole position,' said Josh, draping his arm around

Grace's shoulder and pulling her close. 'I just assumed he'd found a short-cut and would be waiting for us here with that irritatingly superior smirk he usually wears when he's about to be crowned the winner of something again.'

'Come to think of it, I didn't see him after we entered the woods, either,' said Matt, refastening the chin strap of his helmet. Instead of remounting his cycle, he strode into the wooden storeroom next to the lodge and jumped onto one of Ultimate Adventure's quad bikes. 'Maybe he's lost. I'll see if I can find him.'

'I'll come with you,' offered Freddie, running over to reverse another quad bike from the shed. He cocked his leg over the seat and revved the engine, expelling a cloud of grey exhaust fumes into the wintry air. 'Ready when you are.'

'Me too!' said Mia, clearly not wanting to be left behind when there was fun to be had. She leapt behind Freddie and snaked her arms round his waist, her expression brooking no argument.

'Count me in,' added Zara, hopping onto Freddie's cycle and pedalling over to Sam. 'What do you think's happened to him?'

'Nothing,' tutted Penny, rolling her eyes as she stuffed her phone into the pocket of her black jeans. 'This is probably his idea of a joke to get us all as rain-soaked as possible! Theo is so selfish when it comes to competitions – it's always got to be all about him winning the top prize. But you're not leaving me behind. I'm coming with you so I can give him a piece of my mind.'

Penny grabbed Matt's discarded cycle, struggling to climb

on. When she had, she folded her arms and turned to stare expectantly at Abbi and Dylan.

'Well? Are you coming?'

'Don't look at me like that,' pleaded Dylan, his Adam's apple working overtime as the full horror of what Penny was expecting him to do dawned. 'I've just cycled ten miles!'

'I think someone should wait here,' reasoned Abbi, coming to Dylan's aid. 'Just in case we need to summon for help. I mean, what if something awful has happened to him? What if he's fallen off his bike and is lying in a ditch somewhere writhing in agony?'

'I'm sure he's fine, Abbi,' said Grace, smiling at her best friend. 'But that's a sensible idea. We'll call you when we find him – probably propping up the bar in the Drunken Duck!'

'Rosie?' asked Mia.

Rosie glanced around the gathering. All eyes were now on her as the last one to join the party of intrepid rescuers. Should she stay behind with Abbi and Dylan? That was what she wanted to do, because the only alternative was to ride with Matt on the back of his quad bike and that experience filled her with absolute terror. After the recent cooling of their friendship because of Harry's reappearance on the scene, her stomach churned with indecision. She really didn't want to sit astride the mud-caked, over-grown bluebottle as they bounced over the uneven terrain, but the real reason for her reticence was the fact that she would have to mould her body to Matt's in order not to fall off. Could she do that?

'Rosie, come on!' urged Mia, flashing her eyes impatiently at her.

She chanced a glimpse at Matt's face and when she saw the crinkle of amusement in his eyes, heat flooded her cheeks and she relaxed, enjoying the sensation of being in Matt's company once again, not to mention the fact that there seemed to be no awkwardness in his demeanour. One of the things she loved about being with Matt was his constant urging that she grab her courage by the scruff of its neck and experience things outside her comfort zone. Life wasn't a dress rehearsal and every ounce of pleasure should be squeezed from each new adventure. That was the mantra Matt's father had lived by and he'd achieved more than some people would in three lifetimes before the climbing monsters claimed him for their own.

'Scared?'

'No way!'

Rosie shelved her fear, took a deep breath and climbed onto the back of Matt's quad bike, wrapping her arms around his muscular torso and leaning in close. He smelled of fabric conditioner from his damp cycle gear mingled with his familiar citrusy cologne, and every one of her senses sparkled at his proximity. When he revved the engine, a whip of excitement shot through her body and headed southwards. Her thoughts zoomed to the forthcoming weekend when, had Harry not made his unscheduled appearance, she would be starring in the role of Matt's Plus One at Grace and Josh's wedding.

She and Matt might possess character traits at opposite ends of the organisational spectrum, but their humour-filled tolerance of each other's foibles had led to what she had secretly hoped would be not only a lasting friendship, but someone more intimate. Her blossoming relationship with Matt – sealed whilst they'd worked together to save each other's businesses – was responsible for papering over the cracks in her heart caused by Harry's infidelity and was one of the reasons she had been able to turn down his marriage proposal without hesitation.

'This way!' shouted Freddie, taking the lead on their search-and-rescue mission.

In single file, they bobbed along a narrow pathway through the woodland at the rear of the Ultimate Adventures reception lodge. Looking over her shoulder, Rosie thought the building resembled an old wooden steamer moored against the dense forest backdrop; a safe haven amidst an arboreal storm.

For ten minutes, the quad bikes and cycles bucked and bounced on the uneven ground like a procession of kangaroos on steroids and Rosie had to fight to keep down her breakfast. Nevertheless, her overriding sensation was one of warmth and contentment of once again being so close to Matt and knowing that she was exactly where she wanted to be.

'You okay?' shouted Matt, turning his head slightly so she could hear his voice above the drone of the engine.

'I'm fine. More than fine, actually.'

She lay her cheek against his back, arguing with her internal critic that she was making them more aerodynamic, but accepting that an avalanche of emotions had started to tumble through her veins. This is what being with Matt did to her – something she had never experienced with Harry in all the time they had been together. She knew she had to tell Matt how she felt, and she resolved that once they had found Theo she would find the right moment to do just that.

They rode on in convoy for another fifty metres or so until the vegetation grew thicker and the shards of wintry daylight struggled to penetrate through to the forest floor. Rosie's fingers were so cold she contemplated sticking them into Matt's pockets, but before she could decide whether that was appropriate or not, there was a cry from behind them.

'There! Over there!' shouted Josh, veering off between two silver birch trees, their trunks adorned with a botanical garland of holly and ivy. His manoeuvre had been so sudden that Grace had to cling onto him for dear life, her legs poking out at right angles in an effort to maintain her balance. Nevertheless, she had a beaming smile on her face and was clearly enjoy the unexpected trip through the forest.

They came to a halt beside Theo's cycle, its wheels still rotating in the air like an upended tortoise unable to right itself – but there was no sign of its rider.

'Where is he?' said Penny, dismounting her bike and squinting into the gloom, her forehead creased in confusion.

The only sound to punctuate the air was a soft ballad of birdsong rippling through the leaves, and even though the rain had finally ceased, water droplets the size of grapes still pattered down intermittently from the canopy above.

'He can't be far,' said Freddie, jumping from his quad bike and scouring the area. 'Let's spread out. If he's come off his bike at speed he might be injured – he could be unconscious or wandering around disorientated.'

The group fanned out and began to search the undergrowth, not sure what they expected to find. Rosie felt nauseous, not only from the ride but from a deep sense of foreboding that permeated her whole body. Above her head, a squirrel scampered along the dishevelled, skeletal branches and the repetitive coo of a pair of wood pigeons floated from on high, yet the trees bore down on her like a battalion of malevolent warriors. The woodland atmosphere felt oppressive, tinged with the odour of wet soil and crushed pine needles. Her damp fringe tickled at her lashes, and she brushed it away only for it to fall back into place as she tipped her head downwards to scan the thick carpet of vegetation beneath her feet for any clue that Theo had passed that way.

'Where do you think—' began Rosie, but her question was interrupted by a piercing shriek reverberating through the air. 'Was that Penny?'

The hackles on the back of her neck rose in alarm as she met Matt's eyes briefly before he sprinted to where Penny was standing in a small clearing surrounded by a brigade of holly bushes. Rosie stumbled in his wake, sending up a swift request to the guardian angel of cyclists that Theo had been found with nothing more than a twisted ankle or sprained wrist. She just couldn't take any more traumatic incidents.

When Rosie reached Matt's side, the shock hit her like a sledgehammer to the solar plexus. She gasped for breath, drawing her forearms into her abdomen, but she couldn't prevent the dry retch from escaping her throat. Beside her, Mia was experiencing an identical reaction. She was barely aware of Matt and Freddie rushing to Theo's side to check for a pulse.

'Oh my God, is he okay?' whimpered Penny, kneeling down next to Theo, her hands pressed to her mouth, her body trembling uncontrollably as she stared transfixed at the blood oozing from a deep gash across his shoulder and upper arm. 'Matt, Freddie, tell me he's okay?'

Matt removed his jacket and pressed it against Theo's wound whilst Freddie checked his airways.

'Is he—?'

'He's unconscious. Must have hit a branch and come off his bike. Rosie, can you hold this here whilst I call for an ambulance?'

Rosie heard Matt's words but her reflexes had temporarily disconnected from her modem and she found that she was frozen to the spot. With tremendous effort she managed to drag herself back to reality and knelt down next to Matt to maintain the pressure on Theo's wound whilst he removed his mobile phone to call for help.

'We heard a scream, what's going... oh, my God, is that Theo?' cried Grace, grabbing hold of Josh's hand as she stared at the harrowing scene unfolding before her. 'What happened?'

'Fell off his bike,' mumbled Penny, her voice an octave higher than usual, her face drained of every last vestige of colour. 'Matt says he must have been hit by a branch or something.'

But Rosie caught Matt's eye as he finished giving directions to the first responders. Like him, she had seen the laceration on Theo's upper body up close – and it was a perfectly horizontal gash, almost as if he'd been cut with a cheese wire.

Chapter 3

Rosie stared out of the window at the pretty kissing gate at the bottom of the vicarage's garden. She marvelled at how festive the bright red holly berries looked, dancing a jig in the stiff December breeze when such cruelty played amongst them. It was no accident that she and Mia had joined Grace and Abbi in making a beeline for the vicarage, seeking the all-encompassing comfort that was always on offer there.

Dragging her eyes away, she watched Grace set down a flower-bedecked teapot in the middle of the heavily scarred table that dominated the kitchen whilst her mother, Carole, fussed over a plate of home-made mince pies. She supposed that, over the years, the table had seen more than its fair share of confidences and its presence had soothed many an aching heart.

A sturdy, cream-enamelled Aga purred away in the corner, piping warmth and comfort into the room along with a delicate aroma of crushed rose petals and homeliness. Alfie, the family's white Lhasa Apso, snoozed in his basket, one eye cocked for an unexpected titbit. Unlike what had occurred in the woods that morning, nothing bad could happen here.

It was late Wednesday afternoon and under other circumstances they would all have been busy making a start on creating their arboreal masterpieces in the marquee at the Windmill Café instead of waiting for news on how Theo was recovering from his ordeal in the forest.

'Dreadful, just dreadful. Poor Theo,' Carole muttered, shaking her head, her soft features wreathed in bewilderment. 'Have you spoken to Matt, Rosie? Are there any more details about how the accident happened?'

Rosie unfolded her arms and took a seat at the table in between Mia and Abbi, accepting a mug of fragrant Earl Grey tea – Carole's preferred beverage of solace. After all, as the Reverend Roger Coulson's wife, she was no stranger to hearing regular divulgences tinged with sadness, pain and grief from her visitors.

'Apparently someone stretched a length of wire between two trees. Theo was travelling so fast on his cycle he wouldn't have seen it until the last minute. Fortunately, his reflexes were sharp enough to force him to swerve and avoid a head-on collision, otherwise... well, at least he's only looking at twenty or so stiches instead of something much more serious.'

'But who would do such a terrible thing?' asked Grace, her face ivory-pale and her fingers trembling on the handle of her mug.

'No idea,' said Rosie, recalling the brief conversation she'd had with Matt half-an-hour earlier. 'Matt says the police have cordoned off the area and forensics are conducting a fingertip search.'

'What I really want to know is whether this was some random act of violence. Or did the person responsible target

Theo in particular? If so, how did they know he would use that shortcut back to the lodge? They couldn't have! And if Theo wasn't the intended victim, who was? Could it have been Matt or Freddie, or Josh even?'

Grace couldn't continue. Her body crumpled under the strain and she dropped her head into her palms, her blonde curls falling over the back of her hands as her shoulders shook with each racking sob. Rosie's heart squeezed with sympathy as she watched Carole take her daughter into her arms. Grace was the most exuberant, joyful person Rosie knew, but today there were red rings of distress beneath her eyes as she contemplated the contents of her teacup. This wasn't how a bride-to-be should be spending the last few days leading up to her wedding, wondering if someone was lurking about in the village waiting for an opportunity to murder her fiancé or their friends.

'Mum, do you think we should cancel the wedding? How can we ask our guests to come to Willerby when there's a crazy person on the loose?'

'Absolutely not! Don't worry, darling, the police will catch whoever did this.'

'Carole's right, Grace. We have to trust them to do their job,' added Abbi, as she topped up her friend's mug just for something to do with her hands.

'But that could take weeks, or months!'

'Unless—' began Mia, tossing Rosie a surreptitious look from beneath her lashes.

'Mia—'

Grace's eyes widened with interest as she understood what Mia had been about to suggest.

'Yes! Mia, that's a great idea! Rosie, you and Matt have already solved two mysteries. Why don't you join forces again and find out who did this dreadful thing?' she pleaded, drying her eyes with the scrap of lace her mother had produced from the sleeve of her hand-knitted cardigan. 'And if the perpetrator is caught quickly the wedding can go ahead as planned without our family and friends looking over their shoulders and feeling as if they're inadvertent extras in an episode of Midsomer Murders. You *will* help with the investigation again, won't you, Rosie? Please?'

'I'm not sure Matt will be as enthusiastic about joining forces with me this time. Things between us have been a bit... well, different recently. You know, after Harry proposed.'

'But you turned him down. Thank God!' countered Mia.

'I turned down his *marriage* proposal – we're still discussing the business proposition.'

'You can't seriously be contemplating leaving us to go back to London, Rosie. You love it here! You're an important part of the community now, especially after you've singlehandedly rejuvenated the Windmill Café. Who will organize our Summer Breeze parties, or our Autumn Leaves celebrations, not to mention our Christmas Carousel competition?'

'Erm, Graham?' suggested Rosie.

'He'd be useless!' declared Mia, reaching out for one of Carole's iced ginger cookies to dunk in her tea. 'Anyway, our esteemed boss is never here! Hasn't he always found something else more glamorous to do whenever we're hosting the celebrations?'

Rosie had to agree with Mia. Since she'd arrived in Norfolk

the people around the table in the vicarage had become her friends. With their help, she had grappled with her grief over the discovery of Harry's affair and she was now happy to report that she woke each morning with a smile on her face, confident that she had a better-than-average chance that the struggle to bedtime would be devoid of melancholy. She was a totally different person to the one who had arrived at the café, draped in a mantle of gloom that she'd worn as some sort of protective battle armour – and there was one person who had contributed to that improvement more than any other.

Matt Wilson – Willerby's answer to Bear Grylls.

She had loved spending time with him as they delved into the backgrounds of the guests at the Windmill lodges to unearth the motives behind the incidents that had threatened the businesses of the café and the outward-bounds centre. Now she was being urged to resume their partnership to save Grace and Josh's wedding. How could she refuse?

'Please, Rosie,' implored Grace, her face creased with anguish as she pushed back her chair to allow Alfie to jump into her lap. 'Please say that you'll help to find out who did this to Theo.'

'Look, I know things have been a bit awkward between you and Matt these last few weeks,' continued Mia as she finished sending a text and then met Rosie's eyes to push her agenda. 'But, if you want my opinion, he misses you, really misses you. You both just need to talk about what happened with Harry, clear the air and move on. No better time to do that than whilst doing a bit of amateur sleuthing together.'

'And don't forget you've agreed to be Matt's Plus One at our wedding. It'll be the first time he's set foot in St Andrew's church since the fiasco with Victoria running out on him, so you can't let him down too!'

Rosie recalled the steamroller tactics Grace had employed to coerce them into agreeing to partner each other at her forthcoming nuptials on Christmas Eve at St Andrew's Church. It was a day Grace had been planning ever since she'd set eyes on Josh whilst backpacking around Thailand with her best friend, Abbi. Six months later, the two girls had met up with Josh again whilst he was completing a five-hundred-mile cycle ride up the east coast of Vietnam from Hoi An to Halong Bay, during which Abbi had met Dylan who knew Josh through his Extreme Cycling Excursions company.

'I wouldn't miss your wedding for the world, Grace. And, of course I don't mind joining forces with Matt to help investigate what happened to Theo. But I don't think I'll have a lot of time to devote to searching for clues and deducing theories this time. Not only do I have the guests in the lodges to look after, but I've still got the Christmas Carousel competition to organise and supervise, as well as all the catering to sort out for the party on Saturday afternoon after the judging.'

'I knew you'd say something like that,' said Mia, a twinkle appearing in her eye as she slipped her mobile back in her pocket with a grin. 'And I think I might just have a solution.'

The vicarage's doorbell tinkled right on cue.

Chapter 4

'Hello, it's just me! The door was open. Coco! Coco! Come here!' came a sing-song voice from the vicarage's hallway before the kitchen door was shoved open by the nose of a honey-haired Lhasa Apso who rushed in to greet them vociferously before claiming the perfect spot in front of the Aga. Clearly Coco had been there before. However, her owner wasn't so comfortable to be met by a room full of visitors and visibly blanched when she saw the five women sat around the table hugging their matching Portmeirion mugs, all eyes resting on the new arrival. 'Oh, hi. I didn't realise everyone would be congregating here?'

'Hi, Corinne,' smiled Mia, getting up to fetch an extra mug and an empty plate when she saw Corinne was carrying a white confectionery box emblazoned with the Adriano's Deli logo. 'Thanks for coming over. Tea or coffee?'

'Erm, coffee please, black,' said Corinne, nervously flicking the sides of her short bob, the colour of liquid coal, behind her ears as she slipped into the seat next to Rosie and raised her perfectly sculpted eyebrows in enquiry.

Rosie shrugged her shoulders. It was clear that Mia had

asked Corinne to come over, but she had no idea why. She had only met the waitress from Adriano's Deli once before when she and Matt had popped in to sample a selection of their delicious Italian confectionary. She felt the corners of her lips twist upwards when she recalled their brief conversation. It had turned out that Adriano had chosen to employ a waitress who was not only a committed vegetarian, but was also gluten-intolerant and therefore couldn't eat anything that was on offer at his deli. However, that didn't prevent her from enthusing over the myriad of pastries that were on offer, a selection of which Mia was decanting onto a platter adorned with a profusion of the ubiquitous Portmeirion flowers.

'Thanks, Mia. So, what did you want to talk to me about?'

Corinne took a tentative sip of the coffee Mia had made for her, leaving a perfect imprint of scarlet lipstick on the rim of her mug. A waft of her signature jasmine perfume filled the air and her ruby nose stud glinted under the kitchen's overhead lights as she glanced around the gathering.

'Well, I'm sure you've heard about the cycle accident in the woodland next to Ultimate Adventures?'

'Yes, Adriano told me. Awful, just awful. Wasn't the victim one of your wedding guests, Grace?'

'Yes, and Theo also supplied our wedding cars. He and his girlfriend, Penny, came down to Norfolk a couple of days early so he could take part in the stag party celebrations. They're staying at the Windmill lodges – with Sam and Zara, and Abbi and Dylan.'

'What's the news from the hospital?'

'He's going to be okay, thank God,' said Rosie, experiencing a sharp kick of discomfort to her abdomen as she contemplated how the outcome could have been so different. 'Apparently, if Theo hadn't been such an accomplished cyclist, he could have been seriously injured. His wound's been stitched and he's been advised to stay in hospital for a couple of days, but Matt says he's adamant about not missing the Christmas Carousel competition – apparently he's intent on producing a tree worthy of the Rockefeller Plaza!'

'Well, it's a relief he's in such good spirits,' sighed Carole, her kindly face relaxing as she selected one of Adriano's home-baked cannoli stuffed with cream cheese and coated in crushed pistachios. 'And that he's not suggesting the competition is cancelled!'

'Only because he wants his name engraved on the inaugural trophy!' muttered Grace, rolling her eyes.

'But we still need to find out who did this, and why, as soon as possible,' said Mia, leaning forward on her elbows to press her point more forcefully. 'Most of the wedding guests have either arrived or are on their way, so whatever you say, Grace, it's too late to even think about cancelling the wedding.'

'Cancel the wedding? No way!' gasped Corinne, her soft Welsh accent thickening with astonishment at the suggestion. 'Mia, we can't expect our friends to celebrate such a joyous occasion when there's a crazy person running amok in the Willerby woods, can we? Right next to where the reception is being held! What if something else happens? And what if it's Josh who's being targeted? Oh my God, what if it was Josh who was meant to fall off his bike? What if someone *wants* us to cancel the wedding?'

Grace's eyes widened with alarm and Carole gave her daughter's slender shoulder a squeeze. 'Darling, you mustn't say things like that. I'm sure this whole unfortunate debacle will turn out to be a freak accident, and if not, then I'm sure the police will have the culprit under lock and key before the week is out. Your guests are perfectly safe and you and Josh are certainly not being targeted.'

Rosie's heart filled with sympathy for Grace and Carole. The Coulson family had endured their fair share of tragedy over the years and certainly did not deserve to find themselves in such a predicament. She knew the absence of Grace's younger sister, Harriet, who had died of meningitis at the age of seven, would be keenly felt during the celebrations and they could do without the added stress this incident had caused.

'So,' continued Mia, meeting Corinne's wary silver eyes – she clearly suspected Mia had an ulterior motive for inviting her over for coffee at the vicarage apart from the chance to sample a selection of delicious Italian cream cakes. 'Rosie and Matt have kindly agreed to put on their metaphorical deerstalkers again and attempt to unravel the mystery of who in their right mind would stretch a length of twine between two trees that straddle a cycle path! And you, Corinne, could be just the answer to our prayers.'

'Me? Really? How?'

If the situation hadn't been so serious, Rosie would have giggled at the almost comedic look of horror on Corinne's face.

'Well, there's just so much to do, what with organising the

first Christmas tree decorating competition *and* preparing all the festive food for the party afterwards,' began Mia, running the back of her hand theatrically across her forehead, keeping her mahogany eyes trained on Corinne like a puppy desperate for a chocolate treat. 'Not to mention looking after the guests in the lodges. Add to that the investigation of the cycling accident and it all adds up to a lot of work for Rosie. Now, if we could find her a little bit of extra help, it would free up some time for her to resume her role as Matt's intrepid partner. Oh, I mean *crime-fighting* partner, of course.'

Rosie missed Mia's mischievous smirk because she was in the process of demolishing one of Adriano's *Cavallucci* pastries, so preoccupied with relishing the flavours of anise, honey, almonds and candied fruit that her reaction to Mia's suggestion was somewhat delayed.

'Mia, I'm—'

'So, I've had an idea.'

Mia ignored Rosie's frantic gesturing and continued to address Corinne who was busy feeding the final crumbs of one of Carole's mince pies to Coco. When she realised Mia had paused in her soliloquy, and that all eyes were trained on her, her forehead creased in confusion.

'What?'

'If Adriano can spare you from the deli for a few hours, would you be able to help me and Rosie out with the baking for the Christmas Carousel party? Just until the police have arrested the perpetrator, which could even be as soon as tomorrow? And I'm sure Graham wouldn't mind you using one of the *luxury* lodges – complete with heated outdoor spa and Moulton Brown toiletries. Much more sumptuous than your room above the deli,' added Mia, her eyebrows raised encouragingly as she nodded her head in anticipation of Corinne's agreement. 'It's three days at the most.'

'Well, I'm not sure I—' began Corinne, nervously stroking Coco's soft fur as she cast around for an excuse to turn down Mia's offer without appearing to be the curmudgeon who single-handedly prevented the Willerby Wedding of the Year from taking place.

'It's the perfect solution,' added Grace, her tears dried, her face suffused with renewed enthusiasm. 'With Rosie and Matt on the case, this whole thing will be solved in no time and Josh and I can concentrate on having the wedding day we've always dreamed of.'

'No pressure there, then,' muttered Rosie.

She glanced across the table at Corinne, intending to offer her a sympathetic smile; after all, she had often been on the receiving end of Mia's 'good ideas' herself. Under the neon glare of the kitchen lights, she noticed for the first time that their visitor's eyes were red-rimmed.

'Are you okay, Corinne?'

'I suppose so. It's just well you know, this is all very shocking, isn't it? Nothing like this ever happened where I used to live. I have to admit that I'm a bit scared. What if they're still out there, the person who did this—lurking in the trees—watching us all? I usually walk Coco in those woods. Is it even safe to go there now?'

Rosie smiled. 'Don't worry. You'll be okay up at the Windmill lodges. Abbi and Dylan are staying in the shepherd's hut, and there's Sam and Zara in the lodges. Penny will be there by herself too until Theo is discharged from the hospital which probably won't be until the end of the week, and I'll be in my flat above the café. We'll be fine if we stick together. Anyway, we're not even sure that Theo was the intended target.'

'What do you mean?'

Rosie wished she'd kept her mouth shut when she saw the look of horror on Corinne's face. A spasm of guilt sliced through her chest as Mia sent her a withering look.

'All I meant was that the police's investigation is at such an early stage we don't know anything for certain. It could have been an attempt at poaching gone wrong.'

'Okay. I'm happy to help you out with the baking, but I think I'll just stay in the village and come over to the Windmill Café when I've finished my shift at the deli, if that's okay.'

'That would be great, Corinne. Thank you,' smiled Rosie, an upward tick of enthusiasm bursting into her chest. Now that was sorted all she wanted to do was find Matt and get on with the search for the truth.

'Is that a yes, then, Rosie?' asked Grace, the desperation on her face sealing Rosie's determination. 'You and Matt will do it?'

'Hey, what am I getting volunteered for now?' asked the man himself from the doorway.

'Hi, Matt,' smiled Grace. 'Is Josh with you?'

'No, he's volunteered to help Freddie, Sam and Dylan. They're doing a final sweep of the Ultimate Adventures woodland to make sure there are no more obstacles for the unwary to walk or ride into.'

Matt slumped down at the table, shoving the sleeves of his logoed Ultimate Adventures fleece up his forearms in a gesture of irritation at the selfishness of the person responsible for Theo's injuries. Exhaling a long, ragged sigh, he ran his fingers through his hair so that it stood up into spiky blond tufts and made him look like he'd just left his surfboard at the back door. Rosie caught a stray whiff of his signature lemony cologne and was rewarded by the pleasurable twist she always experienced whenever she was in Matt's company, accompanied by the delicious pull of attraction – something that she had missed since he had been avoiding her.

'Any tea left in the pot, Carole? Not had a decent cuppa since six o'clock this morning.'

'Of course. And Matt, now you're here, would you please reassure Grace that it's totally unnecessary to talk about cancelling the wedding. I take it the police already have a list of suspects they want to interview? Do they think this was a random attack or was someone in your cycling group targeted?'

'They're working on the theory that we were targeted. I can categorically state that the wire was not there yesterday. Freddie and I inspected every route through the Ultimate Adventures woodland, including the shortcuts, in preparation for the final sprint of the cycle ride and every one of them was clear, which means whoever did this had to have installed the trap after dark in the full knowledge that the stag party would be passing through the next day. The police have confirmed that if Theo hadn't been such an experienced cyclist, well—he could have been decapitated!'

Gasps of shock ricocheted around the cosy kitchen.

'Oh, my God!'

'Who would do such a thing?'

A curl of nausea twisted through Rosie's stomach as she realised that once again they were dealing with a situation that could have been extremely serious. She had thought that when she escaped the London suburbs to make her home in a cute little windmill in the Norfolk countryside she was headed for a calmer, more relaxed way of life where nothing frightening ever happened. How wrong she had been, because since arriving in Willerby she had been involved in investigating a potentially lethal poisoning, an almost fatal shooting and now what? A potential garrotting? *Ergh*!

'Do the police have any suspects?' asked Mia, her eyes trained on Matt's as she stroked Alfie's ears.

'They've asked for details of everyone who took part in the cycle ride, and their partners.'

'What? Are they seriously suggesting that one of us had something to do with this?' demanded Abbi, spluttering her tea across the table, and, seeing the look of dismay on Rosie's face, reaching for the kitchen towel to wipe up the mess. Unfortunately, this gesture wasn't enough for Rosie and she left the table to go in search of the anti-bacterial spray.

'Well, if Theo was the intended victim, it's a sensible assumption.'

'Oh my God, how awful!' moaned Grace, shaking her head in distress. 'How can Josh and I even contemplate getting married when our guests are being interrogated by the police?

It's not what I had in mind when I said I wanted a quiet country wedding! This is all my fault!'

'It's okay, love. Come on, haven't we got a plan to sort out this whole unpleasant business quickly?'

Rosie caught Carole's eye and saw her nod her head in the direction of Matt, her expression making her intention plain. However, before she could formulate the words to inform him of what Mia had cooked up for them, her friend had leapt into the breach, her enthusiasm sending Alfie from her lap to join Coco next to the Aga.

'We thought you and Rosie could join forces – like you did last time – to get to the bottom of what happened to Theo? Please say yes, Matt. Please say you'll do this for Grace and Josh.'

Rosie stared at Matt, anxiety gnawing at her nerve endings as he took his time to respond to Mia's suggestion. For a few seconds she thought he was going to refuse until his lips curled into his habitual grin with a side-order of mischief. In that instance she knew their previous closeness had not been eliminated by Harry's reappearance in her life, and she knew exactly what he was going to say.

'Another Willerby Whodunnit!' Matt shook his head and Rosie loved the sparkle that had appeared in his eyes. 'At least this time I can't lay the blame at the door of the Windmill Café and its intrepid manager! I'm so sorry this has happened, Grace, and of course I'll do everything I can to find out who's responsible. In fact, I've already had a preliminary chat with Josh before I came over here.'

'Matt! You can't honestly be suggesting that my future sonin-law…' began Carole, her jaw sagging at what she perceived to be a slur on Josh's character.

'Of course not, but he's the only one who knows all his stag party guests. So, apart from Freddie, Josh and myself, there was Archie from the Drunken Duck, whom I'm also inclined to discount, and then Sam, Dylan and Theo.'

'Well, I really can't believe Dylan had anything to do with it!' declared Grace, swinging her gaze apologetically to Abbi who was staring at Matt askance. 'Or Sam, and I don't know much about Theo because I only met him for the first time this week, but you can't seriously be suggesting that he did this to himself!'

'Of course not, and it turns out Josh doesn't know Theo as well as the others, either. He only invited him to take part in the cycle ride because Theo'd offered his vintage Rolls for the wedding as a favour. Apart from Penny, it's Sam and Zara who know Theo the best – apparently he's their sons' godfather.'

Matt pushed back his chair, picked up his plate and mug and carried them over to the sink where he tossed them into the soapy water and left them. Rosie supressed an eyeroll and, out of habit, she rose from the table, collect everyone's plates and mugs together, rinsed and then dried them with a flower-sprigged tea towel and returned each one to its allotted space on the Welsh dresser. Matt could bring chaos to an empty room if left to his own devices, but she was self-aware enough to realise that her perception could simply be the result of her own addiction to order and extreme cleanliness, a trait that had reared its ugly head more often since Harry's reappearance on the scene.

Despite Harry's disloyalty, she had adored working in their little florist's shop in Pimlico, experimenting with ever-increasing creativity in the sphere of bridal floristry. On the other hand, she also enjoyed her gastronomic adventures in the Windmill Café and relished being given a free-rein to showcase the very best that British confectionary had to offer. She loved baking up a storm with Mia at her side, not to mention the possible resumption of what she had thought was a long-forgotten dream – to return to college so she could follow in her father's footsteps and one day, maybe, qualify as a solicitor. She wondered briefly what her sister Georgina would say when she told her she was considering studying A' level law at the local High School where Mia's mother was a food technology teacher.

So, if she accepted Harry's business proposition, it would mean relocating back to London and the chance of resuming her education would be, if not extinguished, put on the back burner. The stress of her prevarication had reawakened her cleanliness demons from their former slumber, so the sooner she made her decision, the better. However, now was not the time for a spot of soul-searching but for gathering facts. Her brain whirred into action and questions bounced around thick and fast.

'What possible reason could anyone have for wanting to harm Theo?'

'I have no idea but we should make a start on finding out.'

'Who are you going to interview first? Penny?' asked Mia, enthusiasm lighting up her face.

'No, I think we should give her some space to come to terms with what's happened, don't you?'

'Well, if Sam knows Theo the best, then maybe we should start with him,' suggested Rosie.

'I agree. Grace, do you mind filling us in on how Josh knows Sam and Zara?'

'Sure. Josh has known Sam since school and they went to the same university; different degree courses, but they shared a flat together. When Josh decided to set up Extreme Cycling Excursions, Sam helped him out with some marketing and promo via the golf club where he works as a pro. Sam met Zara in his last year at uni. They have twin boys, Barnie and Oscar who are having the time of their lives with Zara's parents on their farm in the Lake District. They're a lovely couple. I'm sure Sam will be able to fill you in with anything you need to know about Theo. Come to think of it, perhaps you should ask Zara instead – I get the feeling she doesn't particularly like the guy very much.'

'Why?' asked Matt.

Grace's eyes widened as she realised what she had just said. 'Oh, no, no, I didn't mean that she—'

'Come on, Rosie. Let's get over to the café and make a start on our sleuthing. I can't wait to hear your individual take on what happened in the woods. I have to admit, I've missed listening to your outlandish theories. Though from what I've heard so far, maybe this time you'll be right!'

Chapter 5

Every time Rosie drove through the gates guarding the entrance to the Windmill Café, she experienced a pleasant twinge of homecoming. Christmas had truly arrived, mainly courtesy of Mia, with an exuberant medley of festive decorations. Hand-crafted wreaths hung proudly on the front of every lodge door and plain white fairy-lights twinkled around the windows and on the peppermint sails of the windmill. She had even been persuaded to drape necklaces of holly-sprigged bunting that Mia and her mother had created around the wooden veranda. However, she'd put her foot down at the suggestion they invest in a menagerie of inflatable snowmen to welcome the competitors to the Christmas Carousel contest.

Dusk was in the process of exhaling its last gasp, sending ribbons of indigo and amber across the sky along with a rather menacing cloud of chirping skylarks, their destination controlled by a higher force. An icy dampness hung in the air, and whilst the earlier rain had long-since ceased, clouds hung like bulbous balloons evidencing only a temporary reprieve. Maybe Grace and Mia would get their wish for a winter wonderland at the weekend, after all.

To her right, in the field at the rear of the windmill, crouched the borrowed marquee, its fabric sides flapping in the breeze like a pair of bellows. Her heart gave a sharp nip of gratitude when she saw one of the Ultimate Adventures SUVs parked in front of the entrance and Freddie and Josh helping to unload a consignment of Christmas trees whilst Archie attached each trunk to a huge circular wooden turntable, just like an over-sized Lazy Susan, inside the tent. Once again, Rosie was reminded what being part of a tightly knit community was all about. Every good deed was returned two-fold, and she vowed never to forget that.

Matt's SUV crunched to a halt in the gravelled car park and Rosie drew up alongside him, dragging on the handbrake of her Mini Cooper and scampering in his wake as he made his way to the French doors leading into the café. From the look of determination on his face, he had clearly downloaded his Amateur Detective app already.

She unlocked the doors and stepped inside, flicking on the light and taking a moment to inhale a deep, replenishing lungful of air that contained her favourite aroma – a symphony of disinfectant, freshly baked scones and a light top-note of bleach.

Heaven!

The nervousness that had been brewing about being alone with Matt for the first time since he'd witnessed Harry go down on one knee and propose to her seeped away. She set the kettle to boil, grabbed a selection of the Windmill Café's signature mugs and a plate of the mince pies she had baked the previous day, and turned to face him.

'Matt, I—'

'Rosie, I—'

'Hi? Is it okay to come in? I could murder one of your gingerbread lattes, Rosie. Sam's gone over to the marquee to see if the guys need any help with organising the Christmas trees and, well, I know it sounds stupid but I didn't want to stay in the lodge by myself. Abbi's not in her little shepherd's hut, and Penny isn't back from the hospital yet so when I saw the lights go on in here I thought I pop in for a chat. I hope I'm not interrupting anything? Oh, are these home-made mince pies?'

'Help yourself, Zara,' said Rosie, turning on the coffee machine and catching the smirk on Matt's lips. The fates seem to be enjoying sending distractions their way – maybe it was too early to have the necessary heart-to-heart. 'Why don't you and Matt grab a seat on the sofa over there and I'll bring the coffee across when it's ready?'

'Thanks, Rosie. You're a lifesaver.'

Zara wriggled out of her bright orange padded jacket and tossed her matching satchel, which Rosie recognised as one of Abbi's designs, onto the overstuffed white settee next to the French doors which in summer months were concertinaed back so that visitors could enjoy a meal on the veranda.

Rosie took the opportunity to survey Josh's best man's wife from her vantage point behind the kitchen counter. Her dark brown curls looked slightly more dishevelled than usual and there were smudges of exhaustion beneath her eyes. Rosie supposed that tiredness went with territory of being a mum to twin boys! Her makeup had been perfectly applied though

– a triple coat of mascara, a slick of apricot lipstick and there was a delicious aroma of rich oriental perfume fighting for supremacy with the ground coffee.

However, as Rosie deposited the tray of drinks on the coffee table, she could see Zara's copper-coloured nail polish was chipped and the skin around her nails had been so avidly scratched that blood had been drawn. Her heart performed a flip-flop of sympathy. She knew this was the first time Sam and Zara had managed a weekend away as a couple since their children had burst onto the scene and they should really be relaxing in the spa, enjoying each other's company over a glass of wine instead of waiting for the police to arrive to interview them.

'Mmm, thanks Rosie, this coffee smells amazing.'

Zara gave Rosie a weak smile as she lifted her mug to her lips and took a sip, but it didn't reach her hazel eyes, and before she lowered her drink, a necklace of tears had gathered along her lower lashes.

'Are you okay?' asked Rosie.

'Not really. After what's happened to Theo, all I want to do is go home to see my boys.' Zara's lower lip trembled as she fought to reign in her emotions. 'Oh, don't get me wrong, they love spending time with my parents on their farm. Barnie adores helping my dad with the sheep, and my mum's teaching Oscar how to bake bread. It's just, well, what if the person who did this to Theo is still out there, in the woods, watching us, waiting for their chance to—Oh, God! I can't bear the thought of my children being orphans!'

'I don't think you need to worry about that,' said Matt soothingly.

'Does that mean you think Theo was targeted?'

'I do. And by someone who knew him well.'

'Why do you say that?'

'Theo was the only one of us who took the short-cut through the woodland. If he'd stuck to the path like everyone else, none of this would have happened. The person responsible has to have known that Theo is super-competitive and would have taken the opportunity to pre-plan his route to give himself the best chance of winning.'

'Well, that gives the police an extensive pool of suspects. Everyone who's ever met Theo knows what he's like; always boasting about his last great adventure, or how many trophies he's got in his specially built cabinet, or his impressive handicap at golf, not to mention his amazing achievement of scoring five hole-in-ones. Oh my God! You think it's one of us, don't you? One of the wedding guests?'

Zara's eyes widened as she stared at Matt with incredulity. She returned her coffee mug to the table and dragged the edges of her dark russet cardigan around her chest as if protecting herself from Matt's suspicions. She folded her arms around her abdomen and drew her feet underneath her bottom. Rosie sat forward in her seat and levelled her eyes with Zara's.

'Zara, everyone is upset about what's happened. Grace is threatening to cancel her wedding, so Matt and I have promised to try to find out who did this to Theo so she and Josh can relax and enjoy their special day without all this unpleasantness hanging over the day. But we need your help.'

'My help? Why?'

'Well, we thought we'd ask everyone who knows Theo to tell us a bit about him, just so we can get a picture of who might have wanted to do something like this. Is it okay if we ask you a few questions? Grace told us that you and Sam know Theo the best.'

Zara flicked her eyes from Rosie to Matt and back again, her fingernail-scratching going into overdrive. After a few seconds, her shoulders dropped and she collected her mug from the table, hugged it into her chest and said 'Go ahead. I want to find out who did this too, for Grace's sake.'

Rosie wondered why she hadn't said 'for Theo's sake', but decided to let it pass.

'So, how did you meet Theo?' asked Matt, getting straight to the point and earning himself a glare from Rosie.

'Through Sam. They're both members of a local cycling club in Shrewsbury where we live, and they played golf occasionally. Sam stopped going to the club after the twins were born, and he only uses his cycle to get to work now – he's a golf pro at our local club – so he and Theo haven't spent as much time together recently and that suits me fine. You might think I'm awful saying this, but Theo Morris is not at the top of my list of favourite people.'

'So why ask him to be godfather to your children?' enquired Matt, innocently.

'I don't have an answer to that conundrum. It was the first time Sam and I had ever argued. I've never really gelled with Theo. I find him brusque, condescending and more than a little arrogant. Whenever we meet up he insists that everyone does whatever he has planned, usually organised down to the minutest detail, and woe betide anyone who strays from the itinerary! Once we all went on a trip to Alton Towers – it was supposed to be a fun-packed weekend to celebrate Sam's birthday. When we got there, Theo handed out a schedule and ordered us to follow it to the letter so we could squeeze the most out of the day.'

Zara's eyes had taken on a glazed look, and she had no idea that Rosie and Matt were hanging on her every word and filing each nugget of information away for later dissection. Rosie wanted to ask questions, to hurry her through to the more relevant parts, but she knew it was best to let Zara tell her own story.

'Every single ride was itemised and given a time slot. He'd even factored in one permitted toilet break – three minutes! Ridiculous! You should have seen the notes he had gathered in an arch lever file. It was a weekend away with friends, for heaven's sake, not an arduous orienteering exercise organised for one of his TA jaunts. I really don't understand how the men put up with him, or why. So, yes, it was a huge shock when Sam said he wanted Theo to be Barnie and Oscar's godfather. In the end we compromised and had two godfathers, my brother Jack being the other. Just as well, Theo's never showed any interest in the twins – not that I'm complaining.'

'Could you be underestimating the strength of the bond Sam and Theo have formed as obsessive cycling enthusiasts?' asked Rosie, getting up to replenish their coffee mugs and to fetch a plate of mini chocolate yule logs which she sprinkled with a generous dose of icing sugar.

'Perhaps,' muttered Zara, who had moved on to fiddle with the pearl studs at her ears.

'What does Theo do for a living?' asked Matt, keen to push the conversation on.

'He runs a vintage car hire business; it's mainly weddings, but he also hires them out to TV and film companies and advertising agencies.'

Rosie was surprised to notice a flicker of disgust streak across Zara's expression and her instincts buzzed with curiosity.

'And?' she pressed. 'Is there something else?'

'His accident has nothing to do with me, but I won't lie and tell you that I'm upset about what happened to him. Theo was a conman and a thief!'

Zara blurted out the last sentence with such uncharacteristic venom that Rosie found herself staring at her in amazement. Tiny splashes of red had appeared on Zara's cheeks, but she held Rosie's gaze with determination.

'That's a strong accusation,' said Matt, calmly.

'Well, you would probably say the same if Theo had stolen your grandfather's vintage Rolls Royce.'

'Maybe you should tell us exactly what happened,' said Rosie, offering Zara a sympathetic smile as well as a tissue to dab away the tears that were now rolling down her cheeks.

It was a few seconds before Zara garnered the courage to continue, but when she did the whole story came out in a rush, complete with vigorous hand gestures.

'My grandfather's mental health became progressively worse last winter, but it was still a huge shock when he was diagnosed with Alzheimer's. Okay, so he would never have been able to get behind a wheel again, I get that, but that car was his pride and joy! He bought it in 1959 for £500 and it took him ages to pay off the hire purchase. He was a member of his local vintage car club for over forty years and went to all their meetings until he became too ill to go. His friends still came to visit him at his nursing home, though, and in his lucid moments it was all he wanted to talk about. He adored that car. He drove my grandmother to their honeymoon in the south of France in it over fifty-five years ago, my mum used it for her wedding, so did Jack, and so did I when I married Sam. That car was almost like another member of our family, for God's sake.'

Zara's tears dried and her jawline hardened as her indignation surfaced. She pushed herself upright on the sofa, squared her shoulders and met Rosie's gaze head on.

'Theo'd had his eye on Grandad's car for ages. He'd even asked if he could buy it from him several times, but we always told him where to go.'

'So what happened? Are you saying he stole the vehicle?' asked Matt.

'No, not exactly.'

'What then?'

'Theo conned my grandfather into signing the registration documents over to him. He visited him at the care home without our knowledge, whilst the boys and I were away in Ireland with Sam for the grand opening of one of the golf courses he'd helped to design. It was a couple of months until we found out what had happened and by then the log book had been registered in Theo's name.'

'Why didn't you report it to the police?'

'Oh, Theo's not stupid, you know. As usual, he planned the whole thing with meticulous care. He even recorded his conversation with Gramps to prove he had agreed to the sale. He also gave him some cash which was paid directly into his bank account – not the full market value, but not so little that it would look suspicious. He pointed out that Gramps had been more than happy to sell the car to him, that he'd paid a fair price for it and that was that. I know for a fact my grandfather would never, ever have parted with that car before he died. Never! He wanted our boys to use it at their weddings!'

Tears appeared along her lashes again but Zara swept them away.

'But what upset me the most was the way Sam reacted.'

'What do you mean?'

'Oh, he was furious to begin with, called Theo all the names under the sun and then some, just like I did. He stormed straight over to his house to have it out with him, to demand that he transferred the documents back into my grandfather's name. Theo refused of course, and I think there was a bit of a scuffle – Sam came back with a cut lip. But the very next week Gramps passed away, and, what with the funeral and everything, we didn't have chance to do anything for a few weeks. Sam arranged to meet up with Theo again and when he got back this time he refused to tell me what had been said and told me to drop it.'

'Drop it?'

'Yes, he said that Gramps was at peace and we should move on. I asked Sam what had happened between the two of them but all he would say is that he didn't want to jeopardise his friendship with Theo – that he'd paid a fair price and we should leave it at that. I didn't speak to him for a week! I was livid. That car was part of our family's history and Sam was giving it up without a whimper of objection. I was disgusted with him, but he was adamant.'

Zara flicked her curls behind her ears and Rosie was shocked to see that her insistent fiddling with her ear stud had caused a globule of blood to appear.

'My family is the most important thing in the world to me – more important that a squabble over the car. But I've refused to have anything to do with Theo Morris ever since. I only agreed to come to Norfolk for the stag party because I love Grace and Josh and I'm so excited about their wedding, but I've given Theo a wide berth since we arrived.'

Silence descended on the cosy café and darkness pressed against the French doors turning them into blackened mirrors. Rosie took a few moments to assimilate what Zara had told them and to explore her feelings about what Theo had done.

'So you're not surprised that Theo scouted out a short-cut so he could win the cycle race?'

'Absolutely not! Having a race was his idea in the first place, instead of a fun cycle ride through the picturesque Norfolk countryside, which I know for a fact Dylan would have preferred after his injury problems. It was also Theo's idea to buy a trophy and have it engraved – another one for his over-flowing cabinet! Winning means everything to him – he wouldn't know "fair play" if it danced the Samba naked in front of him. You know who's going to win the Christmas Carousel competition, don't you?'

'Sorry to ask you this, Zara, but would you mind if I asked you where you were between eight o'clock last night and ten thirty this morning?'

Surprise stalked across Zara's face. She clearly hadn't been expecting such a direct question.

'Well, after having dinner with our friends at our lodge, Sam and I enjoyed the facilities. It's the first time we've been away as a couple since the twins were born. We were treating the break as a mini-honeymoon actually.'

'And what time did Sam leave your lodge to meet everyone at the Drunken Duck car park for the cycle ride this morning?'

'It was around six thirty, I think. Yes, because I glanced at the clock when he kissed me goodbye. I went back to sleep for a couple of hours, took a shower and then joined Abbi and Penny for breakfast at about ten o'clock before driving over to Ultimate Adventures to meet up with Mia and Grace where, as you know Rosie, we waited in the freezing cold for the winner to race through the finishing line. Of course, we all knew it would be Theo and that the others wouldn't stand a chance. Only this time it wasn't.'

'So there's no one who can vouch for your whereabouts between six thirty and ten?'

'No, I suppose I—' Zara met Matt's eyes with surprise. 'Oh my God, surely you don't think I pulled on my running gear and hot-footed it over to the woods to stretch that wire between the trees, do you?'

'No, of course that's not what Matt's suggesting, but we need to ask everyone the same question.'

'And you have just told us that Theo was, in your view, a despicable person; a thief who has conned your family out of a precious heirloom.'

Zara leapt up from the sofa, her face fixed with indignation, her hands firmly on her ample hips. Her hair had ballooned into a wild halo of curls from her habit of nervously running her fingers through it. After a few seconds of indecision as to whether to stay or escape, she managed to reign in her emotions and sunk back down into her seat. She inhaled a deep breath and levelled her eyes at Matt.

'As I've said, I didn't like Theo very much, but I had nothing to do with any of this. However, I think I might have an idea who did. So, instead of sitting here accusing me, I suggest you go and question his girlfriend.'

'Penny?'

'Yes.'

'Why?'

'Well, as this is supposed to be a wedding celebration, I thought I'd invite Abbi and Dylan and Theo and Penny over to our lodge for dinner last night. I really wanted to ask Abbi for the gossip on the TV drama she's filming at the moment in Oxford – it's her first decent role after lots of walk-on parts – as well as hear all the news about how her new handbag business is doing. I admit I wasn't looking forward to listening to Theo regaling us all about how everything he puts his mind to is a runaway success, but I thought that if I had a few glasses of wine I might just be able to restrain myself from lunging at him over the table. Anyway, when I arrived at Theo and Penny's lodge to deliver my invitation, I heard the two of them arguing.'

'Did you hear what they were arguing about?'

'Not really, it was quite heated though. I heard Theo shouting "Tell me where you took it!" and then Penny saying "Give me my phone back!". She's surgically attached to that thing, isn't she? Always taking photographs to turn into one of her amazing sketches for her children's books. Barnie and Oscar love her Freaky Foxes series.'

'You think Theo was talking about a photograph?'

'I can't be sure but I saw Penny storm out a few minutes later with her phone clutched to her chest and she looked really upset.'

'Okay, we'll make sure we ask her about it when we talk to her. Thanks, Zara.'

Zara gave Rosie a weak smile as she pulled on her coat and prepared to leave.

'I'm really pleased you and Matt are doing this. Please find out who's responsible so that Grace and Josh's wedding isn't ruined. The Coulsons deserve a break. I assume you know what they've been through with Grace's sister?'

'We do, and I totally agree with you. You have our word that we'll do everything we can, but don't forget the police are investigating too, so maybe they'll come up with something before us.'

'Maybe,' smiled Zara, her eyes filled with doubt. 'Okay, if there's no more questions, I want to get back to our lodge so I can Facetime the boys before they go to bed.'

'Thanks for talking to us, Zara,' said Matt, leaping up to show her out of the café.

'No problem.'

Matt secured the door behind Zara and strode over to the worktop in the kitchen to flick the radio on. The dulcet tune of a Chris Rea classic weaved through the room, and, coupled with the ambient aroma of festive spices from the mince pies, the café took on a cosy, relaxed feel.

'Well, I suppose it *could* be Zara,' said Rosie, whilst she busied herself at the sink scrubbing their empty coffee mugs in a bowl of soapy water before drying them and putting them back in the cupboard above the fridge.

'You think?'

Despite Rosie having her back to Matt she could tell he was suppressing a smile. She was aware of her tendency to suspect everyone immediately after they had spoken to them, but she decided to press on regardless.

'Yes. She has motive, means and opportunity. Did you see her face when she was telling us about the way Theo had conned her grandfather? She was like a lioness protecting her cubs' inheritance. She could have sprinted over to the woods after Sam left for the race; it wouldn't have taken a great deal of strength to wrap the wire around the trees, and then she could have dashed back to the lodges before anyone noticed she was gone.'

Rosie plonked down on the settee next to Matt, groaning inwardly when she spotted an errant splodge of chocolate on the arm of the seat where Zara had been sitting which meant she had to either force herself to ignore it, or suffer the embarrassment of having Matt watch her return to the kitchen for her anti-bacterial spray.

It was no good, her demons had returned with a vengeance and she knew that all the counting exercises her sister had taught her wouldn't work this time so she might as well just get it over with. She jumped up, grabbed a slice of kitchen towel and her trusty spray, and without meeting Matt's eyes, swiped away the offending mess. She realised she had underestimated the strength of Matt's friendship because he said nothing.

'Is that what your gut instinct is telling you about Zara?'

'No, not really,' she sighed as she resumed her seat. 'I like Zara and I know Grace adores her; she's always telling us anecdotes about what the twins have been getting up to. Josh and Sam have been friends since they were teenagers, too. If she wanted to attack Theo, I reckon she would have done it as soon as she found out about the way he'd swindled her grandfather, not waited for months to plan her revenge – she's a *Woman of Action* not of simmering rage.'

Matt grinned.

'Ah, the carefully considered deductions according to Rosie Barnes, Doyenne of Detectives. By the way, those mini yule logs were delicious. I hope there're on the menu for the party on Saturday.'

'So you think we should still go ahead with the Christmas Carousel competition then?'

'Yes! Unless, of course, you want a riot on your hands. Everyone's looking forward to it and I think it'll provide a great diversion whilst this mystery is being investigated. You should have heard Josh telling Dylan earlier about the best way to attach a stuffed parrot to the branch of a fir tree! And I can't wait to debut my own festive creation! I reckon Freddie and I are going to give you and Mia a run for your money!'

'Not a chance!'

She flicked the tea towel she was holding at him and he caught her wrist to stop her. A spasm of heat burned through her skin and a swift arrow of desire jettisoned into her lower abdomen. With his tufted hair and eyelashes the colour of sunshine, it was all she could do not to fall into his arms and kiss him until she was breathless. That exquisite zing of attraction was a revelation for Rosie because, despite the fact that she had loved Harry, he had never ignited her senses like Matt did. Even her fingertips tingled with the effort required not to slide her palms around his neck and pull his lips towards hers.

But none of that could happen until she'd made her decision whether to return to London. It wouldn't be fair on either of them after what they'd been through in their previous relationships. So, fearful that Matt would notice her reaction and suggest they discuss the subject that hung in the air between them like a great big windmill-shaped Piñata ready to explode, she plumped for pursuing their respective theories on the case in hand.

'What do you think Theo and Penny were arguing about last night?'

'I don't know, but it's definitely going on my list of questions to ask her when she gets back from the hospital. Although,' Matt paused to glance at his watch. 'I think we'd better leave that until tomorrow. Maybe you could invite her over to the café for a bit of breakfast and interrogation? Or suggest you help her to make a start on her Christmas tree design?'

'Great idea. Penny's definitely the most creative person in the mix! I really think she'll be in with a chance of winning with Theo out of the way. Oh, I didn't mean...'

'What?'

'I wasn't suggesting that Penny had something to do with Theo's accident just so she could snatch the trophy for once.'

'People have done much worse for a lot less! Okay, I'll see you tomorrow.'

Matt hesitated on the threshold, clearly on the verge of saying something else. However, he thought better of it, twisted his lips into a half-hearted smile and disappeared into the night.

Rosie performed a final sweep of the café, her eagle eye searching for any errant crumb and finding nothing. She switched the light off and slowly mounted the spiral staircase to her studio above the café, her bones heavy with lethargy. As she prepared for bed, she sent up a silent request to her personal Director of Fate that when she woke up in the morning the police would have arrested a suspect so that life at the Windmill Café could return to normal.

If not, she and Matt only had two days until the Christmas Carousel competition, two days before the wedding rehearsal dinner on Saturday night, in which to unravel the secrets behind what had happened in the woods. She prayed that Grace and Josh's celebrations would not be overshadowed by the spectre of a potential murderer floating amongst the chandeliers in the dining room at St Andrew's vicarage.

However, try as she might, she couldn't come up with a plausible theory for Theo's accident and she spent the time before she slipped into the oblivion of sleep not only scraping the bottom of the barrel of ideas, but scouring the wooden layer beneath.

Chapter 6

Rosie slid a batch of cranberry and white chocolate breakfast muffins into the oven and rummaged in the kitchen drawer for a paring knife to peel a knuckle of ginger for a sticky gingerbread recipe she'd inherited from her grandmother. It was barely dawn with only scant wrinkles of ivory light on the horizon over the North Sea, but as it was the shortest day of the year, that wasn't surprising. As she weighed out the ingredients and began to mix them together, she found herself humming a Christmas tune and smiled. Baking really did have a meditative effect and she relaxed and enjoyed the swirl of well-being undulating through her veins.

Unfortunately, her new-found serenity didn't last long because just as she finished chopping the ginger into tiny pieces, she heard the back door click. Without thinking, she spun round, the knife raised in defence, her heart hammering a concerto of panic against her ribcage sending a jolt of electricity spiralling out to her extremities.

Oh God! Was it her turn to be sliced with a cheese wire?

'Hello? Rosie? It's just me, Corinne?'

'Oh, thank God. Hi Corinne,' breathed Rosie, whipping her

arm around her back to hide her offensive weapon before Corinne appeared in the kitchen. She plastered a welcoming smile on her lips, nonchalantly pirouetting on her heels to continue with her task of slicing the ginger, praying Corinne hadn't seen her overdramatic reaction to her arrival.

'Adriano has given me the morning off from the deli so I can come over to help in the café. What do you want me to do?' asked Corinne in her sing-song Welsh accent as she flicked the sides of her ebony bob behind her ears before reaching for a spare Windmill Café apron that hung on the back of the kitchen door.

'Do you know how to rustle up a pancake mix? I thought I'd invite our lodge guests over for breakfast and we can make them into snowman shapes to give them a festive theme. What do you think?'

'It's a great idea, and I actually have a lovely recipe for gluten-free vegan pancakes too, so I'll whip up a mix of that as well, shall I?'

'Go for it!' Rosie smiled brightly, unsure how Corinne planned to make pancake batter without flour, eggs and milk!

'Can I help too?' asked Zara, poised on the threshold, her eyebrows raised in question and her padded orange jacket lending her the appearance of an overstuffed satsuma. Rosie turned her back so Zara wouldn't see her grin.

'Fabulous! Come on in, the more the merrier. There's an apron over there, but before you start could you give Penny, Abbi and Dylan a call to see if they want to come over to the café for breakfast? When you've done that, maybe you could help with slicing the fruit so we can have a fresh fruit salad. I know Corinne will enjoy that.'

'Perfect accompaniment to my vegan pancakes!'

'Vegan pancakes?' said Zara, screwing up the bridge of her nose in distaste.

'Yes. I make them a lot. I'm gluten-intolerant and I don't eat eggs so I make them with porridge oats and coconut milk. They're delicious!'

'Mmm, think I'll take your word for it. I'm not sure I'd be able to persuade Barnie and Oscar to eat them though.'

'Hi, everyone. I thought I saw Zara heading this way. Need an extra pair of hands?'

Abbi appeared, smiling at their culinary labours, displaying a perfect set of white teeth that could grace any toothpaste ad. Despite the early hour, her makeup was photo-shoot perfect and her honey-blonde hair immaculate. Rosie felt like one of the Ugly Sisters standing next to her. That morning, Abbi had chosen a turquoise leather bucket bag with gold tassels to accessorise her outfit of bleached denim jeans and white angora sweater with embroidered powder-blue snowflakes. If her acting career faltered, she clearly had an eye for the next big thing in the fashion arena, thought Rosie.

'No sign of Penny?'

'Not yet, but the blinds in her lodge are down so she definitely came back last night. She's probably having a well-deserved lie-in before going back to the hospital. Poor thing, she must be exhausted after everything that's happened. I mean, it's not every day your boyfriend nearly has his head sliced off and you get grilled by the police about it!'

'Bit graphic for eight o'clock in the morning, Abbi,' chastised Zara, grimacing.

'Ooops, sorry.'

With so much help, a sumptuous breakfast was ready in no time and right on cue, Sam and Dylan arrived on the doorstep.

'We've just seen Penny in the middle of a yoga session on her veranda. She says she'll hop in the shower and be over in ten minutes,' said Sam, reaching for a pancake and having his hand slapped away.

'Okay,' declared Corinne, untying her apron and returning it to its place on the back of the door. Rosie loved working with her new assistant because she was almost as fastidious in her approach to hygiene as she was. 'I'll leave you to enjoy your food.'

'Are you sure I can't persuade you to stay and eat with us? There's more than enough!'

'It's really kind of you, Rosie, but I've arranged to meet a couple of friends for coffee.'

'Well, before you go, why don't I give you a guided tour of the empty lodge? It's really lovely, you know. There's a hot tub, thick, fluffy white towels, luxury toiletries—'

Corinne smiled but shook her head. 'It sounds fabulous, but I really am fine in the flat, honest, and Coco's happy there. I'm just across the road from the vicarage, too, so I can collect Alfie when we go out for walks - Carole's been so busy with all the wedding arrangements she doesn't have time to take him out as much as she'd like. I'll been sticking to the main roads, though, from now on. It's really frightening to think a potential killer might still be out there, planning their next attack.'

Rosie noticed that Corinne's hands trembled whilst she spoke. She watched her shove them into the pockets of her skinny jeans and attempt to fix an expression of false bravado on her face. Rosie wasn't fooled.

'Corinne?'

'Mmm?'

'It's okay to be scared, you know. I'm frightened, too. In fact, I wasn't going to tell you but when you came through the door this morning, I grabbed the potato peeler in case I needed to stab my unexpected visitor. Are you sure about the lodge?'

'Yes, really, I'm fine. See you tomorrow. Same time?'

'Yes, please. And thanks, Corinne, I couldn't have done any of this without your help. Will you send Adriano my thanks, too? I know Christmas is a busy time at the deli. Why don't you take a dozen of my St Clement's mince pies for him?'

'Fab. Adriano loves your mince pies! Thanks, Rosie.'

Corinne's demeanour perked up at the talk of all-things cake related. She zipped her lime-green showerproof jacket up to her chin, said goodbye to everyone, and jogged across the terrace to the car park where she'd left her bicycle, turning around to give Rosie a final wave.

'Don't tell Corinne I said this, but her porridge pancakes are disgusting!' announced Dylan as he munched his way through a second helping of Rosie's snowman pancakes which had been drizzled with a generous splash of maple syrup and a pinch of grated nutmeg.

'I suppose that's the sort of thing you have to get used to if you're gluten-intolerant, allergic to eggs and chocolate, and have chosen a vegan lifestyle,' laughed Rosie.

'Gosh, talk about taking all the fun out of life!' smirked Dylan, pouring himself a double espresso and adding two heaped spoonfuls of demerara sugar.

Rosie saw Abbi roll her eyes at him as he crammed yet another pancake into his mouth, his cheeks bulging like a greedy hamster. Zara giggled at his juvenile antics, which she was probably used to seeing at the breakfast table at home.

A surge of contentment spread through Rosie's veins for the first time since the previous morning. Sharing food with others, even with relative strangers, provided more than just the opportunity to sate the physical appetite. It delivered solace and distraction – something they could all do with an injection of.

As soon as the food had been devoured, Rosie couldn't wait to evict her guests from the café so she could get on with the best part of hosting – clearing up the culinary debris and returning the surfaces to their pristine glory. She didn't want to appear rude, but her reinvigorated hygiene monsters were beginning to scream in her ears, ordering her to grab her cloth and get scrubbing. Just as she thought she was about to burst with frustration, Abbi came to her rescue.

'Need any help with the washing up, Rosie?'

'No!' she shot back a little too swiftly causing colour to rush to her cheeks. 'Thanks for the offer, but I'm happy to do it myself. Why don't you all go over to the marquee and get started on decorating your Christmas trees? There's only two days left before the judging on Saturday. Did you bring everything you need with you?'

'Absolutely! As soon as Grace told me about the competition, I started to plan my entry!' gushed Abbi, her blue eyes bright with creative enthusiasm. 'It took me ages to choose a theme, but I think I've nailed it!'

'And we thought Theo was the competitive one!' mumbled Dylan.

'What did you decide on?' asked Rosie, collecting their coffee mugs and plates together and sliding them into a sink full of soap suds.

She had initially cursed Graham when he'd refused to invest in a dishwasher, citing lack of space, which was true. However, she had to admit that she thoroughly enjoyed the sensation of plunging her hands into a sink of hot soapy water so she could ensure that every single item of crockery and cutlery sparkled before it was stored away.

'Well, as I can do with all the publicity I can get for Biarritz Bags, my fledgling handbag business, I thought I'd use that as my inspiration for my Christmas tree. When it's finished I plan to take lots of photographs to use in next year's advertising campaign. Oh, I can't wait to show you what I've created, Rosie. I've been working on the decorations in between takes of the new crime drama I'm filming in Oxford. A couple of the other actors helped too, so it's only taken me six weeks to make everything—'

'With a little help from Yours Truly, too!' interjected Dylan.

'You've been amazing, darling,' laughed Abbi, leaning over to give him a peck on his bristly cheek. 'I adore every single one of the miniature leather handbags, purses and wallets we've made. They've all been stitched by hand, in a rainbow of colours with matching ribbons so we can hang them on the branches. You should see the garlands I've made from the gold and silver leather tassels as an alternative to tinsel! But the *pièce de resistance* is the wonderful angel, also made from tooled leather, for the top of the tree!'

'Sounds fabulous,' smiled Rosie, grateful that everyone was taking the Christmas tree decorating competition so seriously. 'What about you, Zara? What theme have you gone with?'

'Gosh, nothing as glamorous as Abbi's! Sounds like it wouldn't look out of place in the windows of Harrods! But I have to admit that I had such a lot of fun making our decorations. Mum and Dad have demanded lots of photographs, as well as a live video stream of the actually judging and prize-giving ceremony by the Rev.'

'Actually, Rosie, Zara's had the whole family beavering away like workers on an assembly line; or should that be a Chinese sweat shop? She even roped in her brother Jack and his kids!' chuckled Sam, giving his wife a look of such adoration, Rosie felt her cheeks flush with embarrassment.

'So,' interrupted Zara, grabbing the explanation baton from Sam in her eagerness to tell Rosie about her entry. 'As we're staying in the grounds of a real-life windmill, we decided to use that as our inspiration. We've made dozens of tiny wooden windmills, quite a few pairs of mini wooden clogs and bunches of carved tulips – all of which we've decorated in Christmas colours of red, white and green. Barnie and Oscar have added their own individual touches too; glitter, sequins, little pom-

poms. I even managed to source some packets of edible rice paper in the shape of snowflakes to sprinkle on the branches. It's going to look fabulous!'

'Zara, that sounds awesome!' squealed Abbi, clapping her hands together in excitement. 'Oh, God, come on – let's get started. We're going to have our work cut out to get finished by Saturday morning. I need mine to be photoshoot-perfect. Do you think Penny would mind if I asked her to do the honours with the camera? She's an amazing artist so I reckon she'll know exactly how to get the best angle.'

'Talking of Penny, didn't you say she was planning to come over for breakfast?' asked Rosie, drying her hands on a tea towel and returning her trusty bottle of bleach to the cupboard underneath the sink. She still had the tables to wipe, but already her stress levels were diminishing as her beloved café returned to its sparkling best.

'She must have changed her mind,' said Sam, striding over to look out of the French windows. 'Oh, actually I'm wrong. Looks like she's got a visitor.'

Everyone joined Sam at the window and peered over his shoulder. As soon as Rosie saw who Penny's visitor was, her stomach performed a flip-flop of delight. With as much politeness as she could muster, she shooed everyone from the café and wished them luck with their Christmas trees. And then, for the first time in months, she discarded her bottle of antibacterial spray, grabbed her coat, and rushed out of the café to join Matt who was chatting with Penny on the veranda of her lodge.

Chapter 7

'Hi Penny, I thought I'd bring you a couple of breakfast muffins over.'

'Oh, thanks, Rosie. Mmm, they smell delicious, and they're still warm, which is more than I can say for the weather today. Why don't we adjourn inside the lodge?'

Rosie had to stifle a laugh when she saw the look of delight on Matt's face as they followed Penny into the luxury lodge she shared with Theo. Weak rays of early morning sunshine swept through the floor-to-ceiling windows, highlighting the copper tones in Penny's immaculate bob and picking out the gems in her numerous rings and necklaces that caused multi-coloured reflections to dance around the walls. A faint aroma of patchouli mingled with linseed oil lingered in the air.

Rosie took the opportunity to study the yoga enthusiast whilst she set the kettle to boil. Penny still sported her Lycra vest and yoga pants from her early morning workout; both black, a colour that did nothing to detract from her super-pale complexion. Despite her rotund frame, her limbs were muscular and lithe from her chosen hobby, but that morning her face was devoid of the heavy kohl-based makeup she loved which conversely served to emphasise the depth of her blue-grey eyes.

Penny handed each of them a mug of tea, so thick it could have supported a teaspoon, and indicated for them to take a seat on one of the sofas. Rosie sunk back into the sumptuous silk scatter cushions that Graham had sourced on one of his numerous trips to India, and her eyes landed on an artist's pad on the coffee table in front of her.

'Wow, Penny, this is amazing!'

She drew the sketch pad towards her for a closer look. It was an animated version of the Windmill Café, except instead of being peopled by hungry tourists and locals, the tables were occupied by a coterie of woodland animals; hedgehogs, squirrels, badgers, rabbits, dormice, all in the process of partaking a sumptuous afternoon tea. The attention to detail was stunning.

'Thanks. It still needs some fine-tuning, but I'm thinking of setting my next children's story in a windmill café, that's if you don't mind?'

'Not at all!'

Penny gave Rosie a weak smile, her eyes wide with anxiety as she fiddled nervously with the handle of her mug. From the way she kept glancing at the door, it was clear she was regretting inviting them in and contemplating the merits of making a run for it. Rosie offered her a return smile of reassurance. Unfortunately, Matt wasn't as interested in the social niceties.

'Penny, I know you've already spoken to the police at the hospital yesterday, but would you mind sharing what you know about Theo's accident with us?'

Rosie saw the look of panic stalk across Penny's face and decided to intervene before she had chance to refuse. She explained as briefly as possible about Grace threatening to cancel her wedding and that they wanted to get to the bottom of what happened to avoid the incident ruining their special day.

'But we can only do that if everyone is prepared to talk to us.'

'I told the police everything I know, which isn't much really. I didn't see Theo fall off his bike, and I have no idea who could have set up that tripwire, or why anyone would do such an awful thing.'

Rosie scrambled around for the right questions to ask to get Penny to talk to them, but she discovered her mind was blank. As an uncomfortable silence stretched through the room, a vision of her father floated in front of her. He was holding a copy of his favourite detective story – *Murder on the Orient Express* – and her thoughts scooted back to the long, hot summer when she was eleven and they'd had a competition to be the first to guess the identity of the murderer. Of course, whoever they chose, they were both right and it was still one of her favourite books. The memory of her beloved father and their shared love of solving mysteries galvanised her into action.

'You must be upset about what happened to Theo. Did the hospital tell you when he might be discharged?'

'If it's got anything to do with Theo, he'll be out this afternoon. Would you believe that all he could go on about while lying in his hospital bed was his Christmas tree design, how long it had taken him to source his decorations, and how he was going to get it completed in time for the judging? There's a crazy person on the loose and all he can think about is winning his next trophy! You know, everyone's entering the contest as a couple, Abbi and Dylan, Zara and Sam, Grace and Josh, but not Theo. He doesn't want to share the glory! His words, not mine.'

'How long have you and Theo been together?'

'Only a couple of months. We met in September at a wedding. Theo had supplied the wedding cars and I was hired as a roving sketch artist to capture the guests in pencil, crayon, or pastels as they celebrated the bride and groom's special day. I also painted a watercolour of the church they were married in – it pays the bills.' Penny shrugged, unable to meet Rosie's eyes. 'The bride's father invited us to stay for the evening celebrations and, well—we ended up dancing together until the early hours. I was actually quite surprised when Theo asked if he could see me again.'

'Why?'

'He told me he had recently come out of a long-term relationship and wasn't ready to embark on anything new. I suspected he was still in love with his ex, to be honest. When he spoke about her he had this weird look in his eyes, sort of regret but tinged with something I couldn't put my finger on. It was only later that I realised what it was.'

'What?' prompted Matt, shuffling forward onto the edge of the settee, his eyes fixed on the crown of Penny's head while she contemplated the dregs of her tea as though they contained the answers to life's traumas.

'Anger,' she whispered.

'Anger?' blurted Rosie – that had been the last thing she had expected Penny to say.

'Yes.'

At last, Penny raised her head to stare out of the window at the picturesque scene that had inspired her sketches. Theo and Penny's lodge had an uninterrupted view of the billowing marquee, now draped in myriad twisted garlands of holly and mistletoe and huge elaborate wreaths that Rosie recognised as the work of Carole and her friends from the WI. She could just about make out the bushy fir trees within, only four of which were awaiting a competitor to adorn them with Christmas decorations and her heart gave a twist of pleasure when she saw Mia busy unpacking one of her precious boxes.

Despite the buzz of activity surrounding the tent, Penny seemed to look straight through it, her eyes fixed on an indeterminate point in the distance where the silver-grey of the sea met the transparent blue of the horizon. When she finally spoke, it was as though she was reciting a soliloquy from a play, even the tone of her voice had changed as her emotions tightened her vocal chords and she struggled to get the words out.

'Because we'd got on so well at Mark and Andrea's wedding, I agreed to meet Theo for a curry at a restaurant in Edgbaston the following Saturday. At first, everything was fine – we both love Indian food. Theo told me more than I needed to know about extreme cycling, and the game of golf, before moving on to talk about his vintage car business. After the meal we arranged another date so I could take a few photographs for his website. We decided on a local stately home as a suitable backdrop and we travelled there in style in a vintage Rolls Royce he'd just added to his collection. Theo brought a fabulous picnic in one of those old-fashioned baskets, complete with a chequered tablecloth. I giggled when he produced a silver salt-and-pepper set and a matching candelabra and candles!'

Penny paused and shot a glance at Rosie from beneath her eyelashes.

'You've probably noticed how obsessive Theo is about everything. Even the tyres on his precious cars are as glossy as liquid tar and the picnic could have come from Fortnum & Mason's it was so perfect. Well, I made a joke about his fastidiousness and realised immediately that I had made a mistake.'

'Why? What happened?'

'As soon as the words had left my lips his mood changed so swiftly it took my breath away. He packed everything back up before we'd even cracked open the cellophane on the Waldorf salad and marched back to the car like a retreating soldier. He didn't say a word to me during the drive back to my flat. When I asked him what was wrong he said nothing and just drove off. I didn't expect to see him again. I wish I hadn't,' she added softly, fiddling with the silver chains draped around her neck, twisting them backwards and forwards around her index finger.

'But clearly you did resume your friendship?' pursued Matt, keen to coax Penny onwards with her revelations.

'Yes. He rang the next day, full of apologies, and asked me to go to the cinema with him the following weekend. I was about to decline when he told me he might have another wedding assignment for me if I was interested. I'm just starting out on the wedding circuit so I agreed. You know, the whole time we were together Theo never showed the slightest bit of interest in my family or where I'd studied or about any of my past relationships, and he didn't ask one question about my passion for art. I tried to talk to him about my hopes and dreams, but he always changed the subject to whatever *he* wanted to talk about.'

Penny set her mug down on the table and leaned back into her seat and at last seemed to reconnect with the present.

'I had actually told him that I didn't want to continue our relationship when he asked me to be his Plus One at Grace and Josh's wedding, so we came here as friends. You know, when we arrived at the lodges, for the first time I noticed that whilst he has an easy camaraderie with the guys of the group, he was different around the women. I realised straight away that there was something not quite right between him and Zara. She clearly dislikes him and Grace seems to avoid him like a bad smell. I was beginning to understand why. He's what my mum would call a man's man.'

'But despite this, you still agreed to come to Norfolk with him?'

'I adore weddings – always have. And I've always wanted to explore Norfolk, too. I thought it would provide lots of inspiration for my illustrations, and it has. I just didn't expect Theo to be targeted by a madman and to have to spend hours sitting at his hospital bedside whilst he goes on and on about how he's planning to trounce all the other contestants with his Christmas tree design. The guy's a competition fanatic! When I suggested it was just a bit of fun, he actually ordered me to out of the ward, would you believe! In front of the other patients! I was mortified! Then, on my way out I was ambushed by the detective in charge of the investigation, which completed my day from Hell. I didn't get back here until after midnight and as soon as the police tell me I can leave I'm going to hare it back to Coventry.'

'You mentioned that you thought Theo was still hung up on his ex-girlfriend. Did he tell you anything about her?'

'No, nothing. But I often caught him checking his mobile for messages and disappearing to make or take calls, always whispering and arguing. I once overheard him begging the person on the other end to give him another chance and promising to change. Definitely his ex – a woman just knows these things.'

Rosie saw Matt roll his eyes with impatience before he asked 'Speaking of overhearing conversations, you were heard arguing with Theo on Tuesday night. Can you tell us what that was about?'

'I'm not sure I – Oh, yes, I remember. Me, Zara and Abbi had been to this cute little deli in Willerby that afternoon while the guys were away training for their epic cycle ride. It's such a pretty village that I decided to take a few photographs of the pub, the cottages and that gorgeous kissing gate at St Andrew's church. Later that night, I decided to show some of the shots to Theo. I thought he'd be interested. He humoured me for a few seconds then grabbed my wrist and ordered me to stop. I was really shocked. His grip hurt. Look!'

Penny held out her wrist to show Rosie and Matt her injury. Sure enough, there was a perfect set of dark purple fingerprints across its width.

'He asked to see the last few images again and started to cross-examine me on exactly where I had been when I'd taken them. I was flustered and upset at his weird behaviour, and I have to admit I was a little scared too. I couldn't remember where I'd taken them and he told me I wasn't going anywhere until I'd told him!'

'Can you show us which photograph he was referring to?' asked Matt, indicating the phone that was protruding from Penny's pocket.

'Yes, of course. Although, as I said, I'm not sure exactly which one it was because thankfully Sam and Zara arrived to ask us to join them for dinner in their lodge.' Penny spent a few moments scrolling through a plethora of images before handing her phone over to Matt. 'That's what puzzled me the most. Not only has Theo never shown the slightest bit of interest in my work before – apart from when he wanted me to do those shots for his website – he was especially dismissive of the photographs I took.'

Rosie scooted behind Matt and squinted over his shoulder.

'Ah, look that's Alfie! Isn't he cute!' she cried, a smile tugging at her lips as she saw Carole's white-haired Lhasa Apso chasing a ball across the village green. Grace was in hot pursuit, her blonde corkscrew curls flying into the air like a wild Medusa.

'Are you sure it was this picture?'

'It could have been any one on either side, I suppose. But he definitely paused at one photograph in particular and growled "Where did you take this? Tell me!". I was so surprised at the venom in his voice that I couldn't reply and that's when he grabbed me. I actually wanted to leave the lodge straightaway, but when Sam and Zara arrived, well, I didn't want to cause any embarrassment or spoil the wedding. I decided that as soon as the meal was over I would tell Theo that our friendship was over. But he was charm itself during the meal, really attentive. It was like I'd imagined the whole thing. I can't understand why a photograph of Grace's dog would have upset him so much.'

Rosie watched as Matt continued to flick through the images, taking his time to scrutinise each one in turn. Most of the photographs were of wide stretches of sandy Norfolk beaches, or a troop of tiny yachts skittering on the water, or of the North Sea glistening like a majestic piece of crumpled tin foil under the weak winter sunshine. There were two further snaps of Grace and Alfie, and then a couple of Alfie enjoying a session of canine camaraderie with Corinne's dog, Coco, the two dogs galloping around the village green with abandon. Both the dogs' long coats flew high in mid-leap as though they'd been given an electric shock.

Penny slid her phone back into her pocket and levelled her gaze at Matt.

'What happened in the woods had nothing to do with me. Yes, we had an argument over a few photographs and he did hurt me. But I was going to end our relationship – if you can even call it that – not *attack* him!'

'What did you do after Theo left for the cycle ride?'

Penny glanced at Rosie.

'Well, I heard him leave the lodge at about sixish. I couldn't get back to sleep so I made some coffee and decided to go through the photographs I'd taken the previous day. I wanted to create a sort of montage for Grace and Josh and choose a couple that I could turn into a sketch. Then I joined the others to go over to Ultimate Adventures to wait for the guys to arrive.'

'Does that mean you were alone in your lodge from the time Theo left until you met everyone in the car park at around ten?'

'Yes, but—'

'So you could have left straight after Theo, sprinted to the woodland, set the trap and got back here without anyone noticing your absence?'

'No, I—'

'Thanks for your time, Penny. Everything you've told us has been really helpful. Are you going over to the hospital today?'

'No, I'm not. Theo made it clear he didn't want me there. Actually, I was thinking of packing my stuff and leaving before he gets back, except the police have told me have to stay.'

A splash of sympathy rushed through Rosie's chest. When she had found out about Harry's infidelity with Heidi, all she had wanted to do was escape. To get as far away from him and their flower shop as possible so she could lick her wounds and decide what to do next. She was sure Penny felt exactly the same, yet she was being prevented from voting with her feet.

'Why don't you make a start on your Christmas tree? A

day filled with mince pies, mulled wine and creativity might help to take your mind off everything. And what better way to pay Theo back than by winning the inaugural Windmill Café Christmas Carousel trophy?'

'Thanks, Rosie. I think that's a wonderful idea.'

Penny got up a little unsteadily from her seat, collected her black leather jacket and then paused as she showed them out of her lodge, clearly undergoing an internal struggle as to whether to utter her next sentence.

'You know, it's not just me who argued with Theo on Tuesday night.'

'What do you mean?'

'When the men came back from their practice run, Theo and Sam lingered outside Sam and Zara's lodge chatting. They didn't see me watching them from the veranda. I couldn't see Theo's face because he had his back to me, but Sam's expression was one of horror – his jaw was clamped tight and his fists were screwed into balls at his sides. Theo was actually prodding Sam's chest with his finger and Sam was shaking his head saying "no, no, no" repeatedly. Then Theo stormed off back down to the car park, whilst Sam stayed outside for a good five minutes, smoking a cigarette, his eyes trained on the horizon. He definitely wasn't happy. In fact, I'm sure I saw him brush away a few tears.'

'He was crying?' asked Rosie, shocked at Penny's revelation.

'I know it sounds ridiculous but I'm just telling you what I saw.'

Penny closed the door behind her and pocketed the key.

'See you later.'

Rosie waited until Penny was out of earshot and then turned to Matt.

'From what Zara and Penny have told us, it looks like Theo has no qualms about trampling on people's dreams to get what he wants. That's three people on our list of suspects – Zara, Penny and now Sam.'

'And that's before we speak to Abbi and Dylan. I think I'll do a bit of digging into Theo's vintage car business, see what that throws up. Do you think your Uncle Martyn would mind helping us out again with that side of things?'

'Of course not. It's all he talks about when I call him. You know, he was really supportive when I told him I was thinking about returning to the field of study, although he told me I should skip A level law and got straight to university – until I reminded him that I didn't have the grades. Would you believe he's even offered me a training contract at his firm if I'm serious about qualifying as a solicitor.'

Rosie realised that by talking about her future, she was encroaching on difficult territory. She knew she had a choice to make, and soon, but there were more pressing issues to be dealt with first. She couldn't let Grace and Josh down so all her time and energy had to be focussed on them at the moment.

'Shall we see if Abbi's around for a chat? I've just seen her wheel a huge suitcase into the marquee.'

'I think we need to talk to Sam or Dylan next, to see whether they can throw any light on Theo's background so that when you speak to your uncle you can provide him with as much detail as possible. Actually, Sam's already confided in me that whenever Theo was put in charge of a training exercise at their cycle club his techniques to get the most out of the younger or slower recruits teetered on the bullying end of the scale.'

'And from what Penny has told us, he's transferred that behaviour into his personal life.'

'Come on, let's have a break from all this sleuthing. Freddie and Mia will be wondering where we've got to! What did you say your theme was for your tree? Mia refused to tell me when I gave her a lift over here earlier.'

'Well, in that case I think I'd better keep that little nugget of information to myself,' giggled Rosie. 'Don't want anyone stealing our secrets, do we?'

She slotted her arm through Matt's as they stomped over the field behind the café and made their way towards the marquee. Any awkwardness at their recent separation had evaporated and a warm, fuzzy feeling seeped into her bones. She had the strangest sensation that she was where she was supposed to be, right there at Matt's side, asking questions, following leads, solving mysteries, baking cupcakes and organising Christmas tree competitions.

She wondered if that meant she had already made her decision about her future. She couldn't envisage being any happier than she was at the Windmill Café surrounded by friends who loved her and accepted her for what and who she was, foibles and all. Surely no gold-plated business opportunity could come close to delivering that.

Chapter 8

The sky presented a strange hue of diaphanous ivory light that highlighted the pointed roof of the marquee with a glowing halo. Yet Rosie only had to glance at the dark woodland backdrop to be reminded that the scene was tinged with a soupcon of malevolence. Perhaps the person responsible was inside laughing and joking as they decorated their tree. With effort, she managed to quash the image of Theo's prostrate body lying amongst the decaying leaves and stepped inside the tent.

'Wow, doesn't the place look amazing!'

Rosie paused at the door to inhale a long, steady breath. The fragrance of crushed pine needles was one of her favourite aromas, and in her opinion as integral to the meaning of Christmas as cinnamon sticks, cloves and the smell of warm mulled wine that also infiltrated the tent and added to the festive ambience. The burble of conversation wove its magic around the room, interspersed with the occasional burst of laughter and exclamation of joy, all to the backing track of Jingle Bells coming from an ancient CD player in the corner.

A cascade of intense happiness flooded Rosie's soul and a

broad smile stretched her lips as she glanced at Matt, standing beside her, his face reflecting her own feelings precisely. Matt too had wanted to follow a different course in life; his dream had been to join the police force after completing his degree. Sadly, his father's death in a climbing accident had forced a rethink and he'd stepped into his shoes at Ultimate Adventures without a word of complaint. By his own admission he'd made the right choice and loved every day of the outdoors life with Freddie as his second-in-command. Only occasionally did he contemplate what could have been had life's sliding doors opened in a different direction.

'Come on, let's mingle,' murmured Matt.

The canvas room hummed with activity and every tree had a supporting cast helping to hang the baubles, twist the tinsel, and perch on step ladders to access the higher branches. The gathering for the very first Windmill Café Christmas Carousel competition presented a perfect snapshot of the local community; everyone beavering away at their own creations, but not averse to offering suggestions and encouragement to their fellow competitors; children circling the trees like May poles with ribbons of Christmas paperchains flying in their wake as they snatched a forbidden third or fourth gingerbread cookie from the groaning silver platters.

Only one tree remained devoid of enhancement; it was the last one in the line-up and had been cordoned off by a stretch of red-and-white Christmas tape. Rosie knew without looking at the holly-bedecked entry card pinned to its tip that this was Theo's tree. So far, the most eye-catching of the trees had to be Abbi and Dylan's entry, festooned with the most adorable miniature handbags, purses and even tiny ballet shoes in a kaleidoscope of colours that wouldn't have looked out of place at the Royal Ballet.

Rosie spotted Freddie and Mia working on the Ultimate Adventures entry. She adored Freddie. Not only was he handsome, with a thick shock of hair the colour of a fox's tail and a generous splash of freckles across his ski-slope nose, but he was cheerful, down-to-earth, and loyal to those lucky enough to call him a friend. He was a qualified instructor in rock-climbing and zip wiring, but his true passion lay in his love of water sports which he practised whenever he could.

'Hey, Mia! What are you doing helping the competition?' Rosie laughed.

Mia balanced on the top rung of a step ladder, trying to attach a tangle of fairy lights to the upper branches, the ends of her scarlet handknitted scarf catching on the needles. Freddie stretched up to help her unravel the wire and received a sprinkle of imitation snow from on high for his trouble. He swished it away, reached down into the tub at his feet and sent a handful of the white stuff skyward. Mia squealed and the ladder rocked precariously, causing her to miss her footing and tumble down into Freddie's waiting arms.

For a moment they both stared at each other with surprise, uncertain what to do next, their mutual attraction thrumming through the air.

'Look!' shouted Grace, pointing to a sprig of mistletoe dangling from the adjacent tree.

It was the first time Rosie had seen Mia hesitate before doing something she felt was right. Usually her friend threw herself at every opportunity with abandon, but she was clearly reluctant to do anything to jeopardise her close friendship with Freddie. Of course, she knew Mia had more than friendship in her heart, but ever since Freddie's run-in with Suki Richards at the Summer Breeze party, he'd shied away from the minefield of dating. Rosie agreed that the experience had been enough to scare anyone off, but this was Mia he was holding in his arms – the girl who had loved him from a distance for months, if not longer.

To Rosie's delight, and in front of an appreciative audience, Freddie lowered his lips to kiss Mia, tentative at first until Mia took charge. When he eventually managed to pull away, his cheeks burned, but there was a wide beaming smile on his face as he took a bow to a smattering of applause. Mia positively zinged with happiness as she hooked her arm through Freddie's and guided him towards where Rosie and Matt watched on, exchanging a jubilant Cheshire Cat smile with Rosie.

'Hey, you two! How's the investigation going? Abbi said you were interrogating Penny. Oh, if you need any help with a night-time stake-out, then Freddie and I will be happy to oblige, won't we?'

'Sure!' chuckled Freddie, his eyes bright as he grinned his agreement at Mia.

'Actually Freddie, there *is* something you can help us with,' said Matt.

'Really?'

Freddie's previously joyous expression was replaced by a streak of panic as he nervously scratched the back of his neck.

Fortunately, he now had a staunch defender of his reputation fighting his corner and the look of indignation on Mia's face bordered on the theatrical. She drew herself up to full-height, her hands resting on her hips, her chin raised in challenge.

'I hope you're not including Freddie on your list of suspects this time, Matt.'

'No, not this time, Mia,' Matt smirked, rolling his eyes at her outrage.

'Phew!' breathed Freddie, relief flooding his voice. 'Don't think I could stand the stress of playing the starring role in another Willerby version of Midsomer Murders. Did I tell you about my mother's threat to rally the WI ladies? Would you believe they're planning to set up a new sub-committee called Cosy Country Sleuths after coming to the conclusion that the village clearly has a pressing need of their services?'

'So, what do you want Freddie's help with?' pressed Mia.

'Fred, you were the first person to arrive at Ultimate Adventures on Wednesday morning, can you remember what time everyone else turned up?'

'Okay, well,' Freddie began, drawing his eyebrows together in concentration. 'Josh and Archie came down first thing to help me get everything ready at around six. Then Sam and Theo arrived together at around six forty-five, and I think Dylan turned up in his own car just a few minutes before you at seven.'

'So anyone could have made a detour into the woods before they arrived!' decided Mia, keen to join in the deliberations.

'It certainly looks that way,' said Matt. 'We were all pretty much in plain sight of each other during the race, right up until the moment we entered the woods in fact. If I remember correctly, Theo was way out in front so I didn't see him branch off on his own. Did you, Freddie?'

'No, but there are only two accessible pathways through the woodland; the main driveway up to the reception lodge that we all took, and the shortcut that Theo took. I don't know how he knew about it to be honest.'

'He must have done a recce the day before. It's the only explanation. You know how important winning is to him. Which means whoever did this must have seen him, realised what he was doing, and decided to teach him a lesson.'

'A bit harsh, don't you think?'

'Absolutely. What I don't know is whether they intended to just knock him from his cycle so he couldn't claim the trophy, or whether it was something much more sinister. Did any of you girls see anyone hanging around the woods?'

'No. Sorry.' Rosie and Mia both shook their heads.

'So, who *is* on your list of suspects?' asked Freddie.

'Everyone who's staying in the lodges!' groaned Matt. 'We've only had chance to speak to Zara and Penny so far. Both of them could have left their lodge after the men set off for the cycle race and returned without anyone noticing their absence.'

'And they both have motives, too,' added Rosie.

'Well, if you don't solve the mystery soon you'll have another potential murder on your hands,' laughed Freddie, attaching a bright purple bauble in the shape of a rugby ball to the Ultimate Adventures' tree.

'What do you mean?'

'Before I came down here I bumped into Grace and Carole outside the Post Office in Willerby. They're finalising the flower arrangements for the church pews and for the tables in the village hall for the reception. The stress levels have ratchetted up from low-key anxiety to full-on frenzied panic and Grace is threatening to strangle the person who did this to Theo herself for throwing all her best-laid plans into turmoil. So, all I'm saying is, you'd better find the culprit before she does or Josh will be having a prison wedding. No pressure, Matt, mate!'

Freddie slapped his friend on the back and then turned to Mia, uncertain how to act after their earlier intimacy. But he needn't have worried because Mia grabbed him and planted her lips on his, giggling when she eventually let him go and he stumbled slightly to retain his balance.

'Okay, I can't hang around here decorating trees all day. I promised to drive a client over to the water sports centre in Hunstanton. Catch you later!'

Mia's eyes followed his retreating figure as he jogged to where he'd left his SUV, before heaving a long, satisfied sigh which ended in a slow twirl of blissful rapture. Matt rolled his eyes at Rosie, shook his head, and sauntered off towards the coffee, clearly keen to escape the imminent gushing.

Rosie smiled at Mia, pulling her into a tight embrace, her heart ballooning at her friend's evident excitement.

'I'm so happy for you, Mia!'

'Well, my Christmas present this year has certainly been delivered early! I don't care what's under the tree when I wake up on Monday morning, nothing can match the feeling that's tumbling through me at this moment! I have to admit, I was starting to despair that after what happened when Suki was poisoned Freddie had been frightened off from relationships for ever!'

'I don't think he would have been able to resist your charms for long.'

'True!' giggled Mia, performing another pirouette of pleasure. 'Come on, Rosie, why don't we make a start on the Windmill Café tree?'

Mia almost skipped over to their tree, bent down to select a miniature silver whisk and cheese grater from a pile on the floor and started to hang them on the branches.

'Actually, if it's okay with you, Mia, I think I might pop over to the vicarage to see if I can offer my services to Grace and Carole. Wedding floristry *is* my area of expertise, after all, and it's the least I can do after what's happened.'

'That's a great idea! Don't worry, I've got this. See you later.'

Rosie said goodbye to Matt and made her way to where she'd parked her Mini Cooper. She was relieved the engine started first time and drove with caution to the village, leaving her car in the Drunken Duck car park – with the vicarage bursting at the seams with wedding guests there was no space to park nearby.

She crossed the road and paused for a moment beneath the kissing gate at the entrance of St Andrew's church. In three days' time, Grace and Josh would stand beneath the impressive arched gateway as husband and wife. She really hoped the police would solve the mystery of what had happened in the woods soon so that her friends could sail towards their special day without a cloud of impending doom loitering on the horizon.

Rosie meandered along the pathway leading up to the church. Sprigs of grass protruded from the cracked surface like giant's nasal hair, dense rhododendron bushes crowded on either side, and an unpleasant aroma of damp, rotting vegetation met her nostrils. A sudden rustle of leaves caused her to pause, her senses on high alert. Insidious fingers of fear raked at her skin and caused goosebumps to scamper across her forearms.

Was the person who had arranged Theo's accident watching her from the depths of the foliage at that very moment?

She squinted through the veil of shadow to her left, a bolt of shock alighting her veins when a pair of shining black pearls stared straight back at her. She broke into a sprint, and when she arrived on the vicarage doorstep, she pressed the doorbell with excessive alacrity.

'Hi Rosie, great to see you. What's the matter?' asked Carole, her forehead creasing in concern. 'Why are you out of breath? Come in. Come in. Oh, I see you've brought Constance with you.'

'Constance?'

'Our friendly neighbourhood cat. Look.'

Rosie almost laughed out loud when she saw the coal-black cat strolling towards them with a look of haughty disdain written across its feline features.

'Oh, yes. Erm, I was wondering whether you wanted any help with the wedding flowers?'

'Ah, thanks, Rosie. That's music to my ears!'

'Well, I *have* designed a fair few bouquets in my time.'

'And for celebrities, too, I hear!'

As soon as she stepped over the threshold, Rosie was once again enveloped in the familiar warm mantle of comfort. The air smelled of home-baked bread, furniture polish and freshly ground coffee beans. Grace, Abbi and Corinne sat at the kitchen table, a jumble of blooms, foliage and spools of pale pink ribbon piled high in the centre. Grace was experimenting with blocks of green oasis that had been cut to fit her mother's pretty Portmeirion bowls, and a set of china teacups had also been pressed into service as flowerpots. The whole scene was a neat synopsis of village life – welcoming, relaxed, with the promise of a decent cup of coffee and a sweet treat.

'Rosie! Am I glad to see you. I have no idea what possessed me to think we'd be able to handle the flower arrangements ourselves! Are you sure you don't mind?'

'Not at all. In fact, I'm really looking forward to it. I adore flowers.'

'Oh my God! I completely forgot! Forgive me.'

'What? Why?'

'Well, I know you still haven't decided whether to take Harry upon his offer. What if helping me with my wedding bouquets makes you yearn for your former passion and you decide to leave us, and your job at the Windmill Café, and dash back to the bright lights of the metropolis? It'll be all my fault—'

'Grace, Grace,' Rosie laughed. Freddie had been right, the stress levels in the Coulson household were rising. However, she had no desire to get into a discussion about where her future lay, whether that be Pimlico or Willerby. 'I think you've got enough to worry about without adding me to your list. Okay, so what sort of design are you looking for?'

The women spent the next two hours following Rosie's lead as she demonstrated a selection of posies that could be hung on the ends of the pews and then recycled as table decorations. The fragrance of the flowers, mingled with Carole's Estée Lauder perfume, set the scene perfectly for an afternoon of gossip about cupcakes, confetti and couture. Rosie filled them in on the romance that had been played out in front of her starring Mia and Freddie and everyone agreed that it was about time the two got together, that it would have probably happened much sooner had it not been for the events at the Summer Breeze party.

When everyone had made five posies each, with Rosie concentrating on a larger, more elaborate display for the top table, Carole insisted on laying each of the arrangements on a huge wooden tray and then scrutinising the results like an art critic considering the Turner prize. Rosie wouldn't have been surprised if she had scored them out of ten!

'You are an absolute genius, Rosie. Thank you for coming to our rescue.'

'Gosh, no thanks required, I've had fun.'

'Okay, it's coffee and carrot cake all round!' declared Carole, making herself busy with the kettle.

'Not for me, I think I'd better be making tracks,' said Corinne. 'Don't want to be late.'

'Thanks, Corinne.'

'No problem. Bye everyone.'

Corinne grabbed her denim jacket, called Coco to heel, and slammed the front door of the vicarage behind her with a resounding crash.

'Where's Corinne off to?' asked Rosie, scanning the sink for the bleach so she could help Carole to wipe the table and kitchen benches down before she indulged in a slab of her host's signature bake.

'Freddie's offered to take her for a windsurfing lesson this afternoon,' said Carole, setting the cafetière down on the table. 'Apparently, she adores water sports and was a member of her local rowing club before she arrived in Norfolk. The two of them went kayaking last week and I think they've got plans to hire a boat when the weather improves. She's slotted in to village life rather well, don't you think?'

'She's lovely!' declared Grace, her demeanour much more relaxed now the issues with the flowers had been resolved. 'You should see the Italian *buffet dei dolci* she's made for the evening reception.'

'What about your wedding cake?'

'It's spectacular, isn't it, Abbi? Exactly the design I wanted! It's hidden in the dining room, though. It's safer there – no risk of any freak accidents.'

'Or poisonings,' muttered Carole, not altogether joking. She patted her curls, freshly highlighted with golden strands in preparation for her daughter's wedding, and straightened the skirt of her flower-sprigged tea dress before slicing the cake.

'So, everything is sorted! Now all you need to do, Rosie, is solve this woodland mystery and normal service can be resumed. I have every faith in you and Matt, but I'm sure you won't say no if I ask Dad to request a little help from a higher authority?'

'Not at all,' smiled Rosie. 'We need all the help we can get!'

Chapter 9

Rosie jogged back to her car, her mind swirling with ideas for new recipes to try out at the Windmill Café when it re-opened full-time in April. However, she also found her thoughts lingering on how much she had enjoyed creating the bespoke wedding posies and table arrangements for Grace and Josh's wedding. She smiled to herself when she recalled the floristry competitions she had won whilst in London, and the weird and wonderful prizes she had received for her efforts – a year's supply of fertilizer anyone?

As she scrambled in her pocket to locate her car keys, she became aware of the gnaw of anxiety in the pit of her stomach caused by the fact that unless she and Matt focused all their energies on discovering who had set the trap in the woodland, then the happy occasion would be spoiled. They needed to talk to Theo as soon as possible and if he wasn't going to be discharged from hospital the next day, then they needed to take a trip to Norwich to see him. They also still had to talk to Dylan and Sam. She had purposely left Josh off her list of potential suspects – there was no way he would have done anything to jeopardise his own wedding!

She found her keys and was about to open the driver's door of her little Mini when her heart gave a leap of surprise.

'Hi Rosie, how's Grace holding up?'

'Oh, hi Sam. Well, she's still upset about this whole episode in the woods, but she's much more relaxed now than when I arrived a few hours ago. As far as the wedding is concerned, though, I think everything is on track; the flowers arrangements have been finalised, the wedding favours and place cards are done, and the cake is sorted. Actually, I was just thinking about coming to see you at the lodge. We should—'

'Hello, Sam, hi Rosie. Are you on your way in to the Drunken Duck or on your way out?' asked Matt, striding over to offer Sam his palm and deposit a tantalisingly brief kiss on Rosie's cheek. She tried to ignore the ripple of interest that shot down her spine and lodge somewhere deep in her lower abdomen.

'Oh, no, I was just—'

'Let me buy you a drink,' offered Matt, as usual taking advantage of an unexpected stroke of luck.

'What's the local beer like?'

'I think you'll love it.'

They piled into the Drunken Duck. Matt paused at the bar to give his order to Archie while Rosie led Sam into the room at the rear. It was five o'clock and most of the pub's patrons had either left for the day or hadn't yet arrived, so they had the place to themselves.

Rosie loved the snug, and that day it was suffused in a dusty light that gave the whole room a sepia feel. Archie had chosen to furnish it with an eclectic mix of antique and modern styles, from the benches and tables fashioned from old church pews to the framed photographs and old maps of local landmarks. An orphaned copy of that day's newspaper rested on the mantelpiece waiting to be adopted, and there were tattered beer mats galore.

The chaos should have caused Rosie's disorder hackles to rise and yet they didn't. Far from it. When she sunk down into the leather banquette next to the roaring fire, she relaxed and allowed the comfortable ambience to perform its magic. This was a space she could happily spend hours in, relishing the soft murmur of conversation, the gentle clinking of glasses, the scent of yeasty local craft ales.

However, a quiet drink was not on the agenda and she resolved to sharpen her wits so that she could extract the salient facts from Sam without causing him to beat a hasty retreat.

'Mmm, you're right, Matt. This beer's good,' announced Sam after swallowing half a pint of Wherry in one go. 'Boy, did I need that. I've spent the whole afternoon being attacked by a barrage of pine needles whilst Zara hums and haas about achieving the perfect balance between symmetry and colour coordination, or some such malarkey.'

Sam inspected the backs of his hands where numerous scratches evidenced his complaints.

'She's still down there, in the marquee, tweaking every branch and rearranging every bauble. Anyone would think Kirstie Allsopp was on her way with a battery of TV cameras! She nearly snapped my head off when I suggested we adjourned for a drink at the Drunken Duck or treated ourselves to a coffee at Adriano's deli! I suppose it keeps her mind off worrying about the boys, not to mention this fiasco over Theo's accident. Do you think there's any way it could have been an accident? Someone put up an animal trap and made an error of judgement about the height?'

'No, I don't think so,' replied Matt, replacing his pint of Guinness on the beermat and running his tongue along his upper lip to collect the froth. 'Freddie and I swept the area behind the Ultimate Adventures lodge the night before the race and that wire wasn't there then, I'm certain of it. Someone put it there specifically for our cycle ride.'

'So any one of us could have been the victim!'

'True. We really need to talk to Theo about that.'

Rosie knew Matt had stopped himself from going on to say that he suspected Theo had surveyed the area the previous day too; it was the only way he could have known about the shortcut.

As she sipped her glass of Merlot, she took a few moments to consider their companion. At six-foot-two and with a slender, well-honed physique, Sam Vardy projected a charismatic image. His short blond hair had been teased into a perfect quiff at his forehead and his clean-shaven face still displayed a light tan from his recent trip to the golf courses of Dubai. His crisp, baby pink shirt, open at the neck to reveal a smattering of golden hairs, was Jermyn Street quality and Rosie suspected the diamond cufflinks at his wrists – each depicting a miniature set of golf clubs – were the real thing.

'Sam, we all want to get to the bottom of what happened

to Theo, especially Josh and Grace, so do you mind if Rosie and I ask you a few questions?'

'Of course not. The sooner the imbecile is caught the better!'

'Thank you. I wonder if you could start by telling us how well you know Theo?'

'We met at our local cycling club – mutual interests built up our friendship, I suppose. I don't go there as often as I used to but we've kept in touch.'

Sam shrugged his shoulders and flashed a smile at Rosie before slotting his palms into his trouser pockets and crossing his ankle over his thigh so he could lean back in his seat in a calm, nonchalant manner. Rosie thought he was trying too hard to be composed and she had the strangest feeling he was hiding something; it was a revelation that she enjoyed. It meant she was getting better at this sleuthing business and she knew her beloved father would have been immensely proud of her. She wasn't sure whether Matt had noticed, so she decided to ask her own questions with an assertiveness she knew Sam would respond to.

'If you got on so well why were you arguing with him outside your lodge on Tuesday night?'

Bingo, she thought as she saw his face take on the colour of overworked putty.

'Oh, you know – just general stuff. Anyway, I think we were chatting, not arguing.'

'Well, your voices were definitely raised, and apparently you were heard saying "no, no, no". Never mind, I suppose I'll just have to pass the information on to the police so they can ask you about it themselves.'

'No! Erm, no, there's no need to do that!' Sam's eyes widened and a nervous tic appeared just above his left cheek. He removed his ankle from his thigh so he could lean forward, placing his elbows on his knees, the remainder of his pint of Wherry left untouched. 'Okay, okay, I'll tell you, but does the information have to go any further that this room?'

'We can't give you any guarantees,' said Matt before Rosie could respond.

Sam's previous display of macho bravado seeped from his body. He rubbed his palm over his face then laced his fingers on the table in front of him to prevent them from shaking. He took a deep breath before he spoke, his throat tightening around each word.

'You know what I do for a living – I'm a golf Pro at one of the West Midlands' most prestigious golf clubs, but I've also been fortunate enough to be consulted on the design and construction of a few championship-quality golf courses, both here in the UK and abroad. It's an amazing opportunity, something that was beyond my wildest dreams when I was at university. My brother Marcus and I have been obsessed with the game since we were five years old. He's a Pro, too, at an exclusive club in Dubai – it was Marcus who put in a word for me as a design consultant for a new course out by the airport. It's taken two years to complete but it's been worth every setback – it's a true championship course in every sense of the word!'

'What has this got to do with Theo's accident?' asked Rosie, keen to divert the conversation away from bunkers and fairways.

'I'm getting there.' Sam pulled his lips between his teeth and began to chew at the skin on the inside of his cheeks. His whole body had started to tremble. 'The Dubai project meant that I had to be away from home for weeks on end. At first, I spent all my spare time working on my swing with Marcus, or on the tennis court, or at the gym. But I was bored and I missed Zara and the boys.'

Rosie watched Sam swallow down his discomfort and realised immediately what was coming.

'I don't know how it happened, but there was this female golf Pro at the club where Marcus worked, a real party girl. We went out for a few drinks and, one thing led to another – Well, do I have to spell it out? We had a relationship. I managed to keep it quiet and we were especially careful when we were around Marcus, but this one weekend Theo flew out unannounced, hoping to squeeze in a couple of rounds, and he caught us in a compromising position.'

Sam concentrated on his clenched hands, taking a few moments to compose himself. Beads of perspiration appeared on his forehead and his eyes had taken on a wary look.

'Don't get me wrong. I totally deserved the blasting Theo gave me. He was livid – and rightly so. He's godfather to our twins! He kept going on and on about honour and integrity and respect. Of course, I terminated my relationship with Natasha immediately and swore to Theo that I would never do anything to jeopardise my family again. In return he promised he wouldn't tell Zara.'

'Is that what you were arguing about on Tuesday night?'

'Sort of.'

Sam grabbed his glass and finished his beer in one gulp, wiping his lips with the back of his hand, and studiously avoided looking in Rosie's direction.

'What do you mean by "sort of"?'

'I'm not proud of myself, but Theo had discovered – I have no idea how – that I spent a weekend up at Gleneagles with Natasha a few months back. It was a celebration bash for everyone who'd been involved in the Dubai project. I'd had a barrelful of whiskey and I succumbed to temptation. It was a one-off, but of course I'd broken the promise I'd made to Theo, not to mention Zara and the boys.'

Sam began to fiddle with the strap of his Tag Hauer watch strap, his fingers shaking.

'This time he was determined to tell Zara. He kept saying that he'd already given me a chance to rectify my disgraceful behaviour and I'd chosen not to take it. He said it was his duty to disclose my indiscretions. I begged him to think about the impact his revelation would have on the boys but he refused to listen. The only thing I managed to get him to agree to do was to wait until after Josh and Grace's wedding. I know how much Zara adores Grace and I didn't want what I'd done to spoil their day. I do love Zara.'

'And when you were overheard arguing with Theo, you were pleading with him to remain silent?'

'Yes.'

'So, you have ample motive for wanting to harm Theo, maybe to shut him up for good?'

'No! Well, yes, I wanted him to keep quiet about what I'd done, but I would never do anything to hurt him! We've been friends for years, before I was married we spent most summer weekends cycling all over the country. But Zara never liked him, so our friendship has cooled a bit over the last few years.'

'Did you cheat on your wife before you had children?'

'No!' Sam glared at Matt. 'What do you take me for? It was a temporary blip when I was away from my family that I've regretted ever since.'

'Did you think Theo being godfather to your children would secure his silence about your affair?'

'Maybe, but even if I did, I had nothing to do with his accident!'

'Thank you for your honesty,' said Rosie, a maelstrom of emotions swirling through her stomach. She couldn't believe what Sam had just confessed, and whilst he looked genuinely contrite, she had trouble feeling sorry for him.

'Okay, well, I think I'd better get back to the lodge. Zara will be wondering where I've disappeared to.'

Sam almost sprinted from the snug, his shoulders hunched under the burden of guilt, and a good few inches shorter than when he'd arrived.

'Oh, God, yet another member of the advance wedding party with a reason for wanting Theo to suffer!' groaned Matt. 'I don't want to broadcast the details of his personal life, or to cause any unnecessary heartache to Zara unless we absolutely have to. What do you think?'

'I agree, but clearly Theo didn't feel the same way.'

Another random piece of the jigsaw puzzle had been collected, she thought, but obviously they were slotting them in in the wrong order because the picture was no clearer than when they had started their investigation. Okay, they had a list of characters that had been invited to attend Grace and Josh's wedding, but as yet they didn't know the plot-line, let alone the epilogue, and time was running out. Unless they unmasked the perpetrator in the next forty-eight hours Grace's hope of having a wedding day free from anxiety was resting on nothing but quicksand.

Rosie raised her eyes to meet Matt's and experienced a surge of pleasure. There was no one else she would rather spend her free time with, even if they seemed to be making a habit of investigating mysteries, and it was time to talk to him about Harry's offer, to explain her deep-seated fear of losing her home again, how she was haunted by what had happened in her childhood and the insecurity her mother's breakdown had wreaked on the family still grieving after her father's death. Choosing to stay at the café was a risky decision, especially if the food poisonings, shootings and cycle accidents continued. Could she contemplate flying into her future without the benefit of a safety net?

Chapter 10

Friday morning's dawn chorus was lacklustre and feeble, as though the birds were expressing their disapproval of the grey, drizzly weather. Against all the odds, Rosie had slept well and she leapt from her bed to rinse away any remaining cobwebs in the shower. As she towel-dried her voluminous hair, she took a few moments to enjoy the view from her bedroom window. The silver-grey majesty of the North Sea rippled in the distance like a sheet of mercury under the leaden skies, whilst the undulating fields in the foreground were colourless and melancholic.

She couldn't believe Christmas Eve was only two days away, which also meant that so was Grace and Josh's wedding, and the bottom fell from her stomach like a penny down a well as she contemplated the list of things she needed to accomplish before then. She scoured her brain for inspiration, hoping that her good night's sleep had allowed the little grey cells to work subconsciously on the conundrum whirling around her brain. But, of course, she drew a blank.

As she applied a slick of mascara, her thoughts lingered on her father, his smiling face encouraging her to consider as many theories and scenarios as possible. Oh, what she wouldn't give to have him next to her, sitting at her dressing table, urging her to keep plodding on, helping her to dissect the facts they had gathered so far. But he wasn't there; he hadn't been there for fifteen years and his loss still hurt.

'Rosie? Are you up there?'

Rosie smiled. She couldn't indulge her sadness for long when she had a friend like Mia.

'I am. Come on up.'

'Hi. Is the kettle on?'

'Of course! Isn't it always?'

'I take it you and Matt are no nearer to finding out who sneaked into the woods in the dead of night and rigged up that cheese wire to garrotte any unsuspecting passing cyclist?'

'Correct.'

Rosie pulled a face when she sipped her coffee, realising she had forgotten to add milk. The taste of strong black coffee lingered on her tongue like dark molasses.

'Well, don't take this the wrong way, but you look exhausted.'

'Cheers, Mia. Just what I was hoping to hear this morning.'

'When was the last time you took some time out to enjoy yourself? To do something just for you; not running the café, not organising the Christmas tree competition, not designing wedding bouquets, and not starring in the lead role of private detective?'

'I love doing all those things.'

'All I'm saying is that you have to take a break, even if it's just for a couple of hours. You can't possibly function properly when you're tired. Sometimes, when you take a step back, you see things you wouldn't normally see when you're submerged beneath all the detail.'

'What do you have in mind?'

Rosie groaned inwardly when she saw the triumphant smile on Mia's face and wished she had put up more of a fight. There was still so much to do – mainly making sure the contestants had everything they needed before Reverend Coulson arrived sporting his judge's badge on Saturday lunchtime.

'Walk this way, Miss Barnes. Oh, and you might want to grab a warm jacket, and maybe a bobble hat, a scarf and some gloves.'

Rosie shot a worried glance across at Mia whose eyes sparkled with mischief as she shook her head to indicate she had no intention of spilling the beans. She followed her friend, noticing for the first time the outrageously over-the-top green elf boots she was wearing – complete with sleigh bells on the tassels. It wasn't long before she realised that Mia was leading her to the car park where she saw Matt's SUV chugging at rest.

'Okay, so you two kids have fun, and when you get back I'll have every one of our competitors ship-shape and ready to showcase their amazing trees tomorrow.'

'Mia, I—'

Her heart ballooned with gratitude, not only for Mia's unwavering support, but for every single one of the friends she had made in Willerby. Carole, Roger and Grace, Freddie and Archie, but most of all Matt who seemed to have the inherent knack of knowing exactly when to provide a diversion from the hectic hustle and bustle of life as a café and holiday site manager. She sent up a missive of thankfulness to her guardian angel that she had been bestowed with such good fortune.

'Thanks, Mia.'

She suddenly couldn't get any more words out because her throat had tightened with emotion. Mia nodded in silent understanding, swivelled on her heels and sashed towards the marquee humming a rendition of Do They Know It's Christmas.

'Hi Matt. So, what's Mia organised for us?'

'Wait and see!'

Matt beamed at her, and instead of the gesture putting her mind at rest it had the opposite effect. She knew him well enough now to suspect that the gleam in his eyes meant she was about to be the victim of another one of his 'give everything a go' ripostes. She thought of arguing with him but decided to go with the flow – an altogether new experience for her.

Unfortunately, the meteorological gods were playing for the opposing team that morning and the ever-present drizzle painted a gloss on the slate roof tiles of the cottages in the village blurring their sharp edges. But she was determined to ignore the weather and enjoy whatever Matt had planned for them despite the niggle of nerves in the base of her stomach because she knew it would probably involve some sort of strenuous activity.

She settled into her seat and surveyed her companion from beneath her lashes. In profile, Matt was as attractive as ever in his black jeans and Ultimate Adventures logoed sweater. The collar was open to reveal a smattering of chest hair and a ripple of desire joined her apprehension. It occurred to her that whenever she sat next to Matt Wilson her emotions churned uncontrollably, whether that was an overflow of discomfort whenever she visited him in the messy kitchen at his office, pleasure when he had suggested they work together on the investigation, or the concoction of nervousness and sexual attraction that was whipping through her veins at the present moment. Being with Matt was hazardous whichever way she looked at it, and she had an inkling that the situation was only going to magnify over the next few hours.

Her eyes lingered on the way his hand draped across the steering wheel; sure, relaxed, confident. Why had he insisted on keeping the activity they were on their way to a secret? But she knew the answer – Matt had expected her to refuse, to plead a more urgent engagement. And he was right. After all, she was a sunshine addict, not a rain dancer! Panic started its insidious coil around her abdomen and she began to feel lightheaded.

'Matt, I really—'

'What's the matter? Your face looks like a slab of my mother's pastry.'

'I think your idea of having fun and mine reside at opposite sides of the Richter scale. Can't we just—'

'Are you telling me that you're frightened of trying something new? Aren't you always telling me that you love experimenting.'

'In the kitchen! With new recipes and ingredients! Or with

the most exotic flowers and tropical foliage I can get my hands on! Yes!'

Matt chuckled. 'Ah, there she is! The Rosie Barnes I know and love!'

Rosie gawped at what he had just said but the SUV took a sudden sharp left through the gates of Ultimate Adventures and she had to grab onto her seat to steady herself and the moment was lost. When they arrived at the reception lodge, the next, and more welcome sensation in her kaleidoscope of emotions was relief. Although an hour on the climbing wall would not have been her first choice of activity, it beat the spots off anything airborne.

'Are you ready to indulge your inner ape?'

'Ape? What are you talking about?'

Rosie followed Matt's eyes into the leafy canopy overhead and the bottom dropped out of her stomach.

'No way! No, absolutely not!'

'Hi Rosie,' called Grace, emerging from the reception with Josh and Freddie in her wake; all three of them were dressed for the activity Matt had planned in safety helmets, and knee and elbow pads. 'I wasn't sure whether Matt would be able to persuade you to join us. I'm glad he did – this is definitely going to be the best stress-busting activity ever!'

Rosie stared at Grace, struggling to formulate an answer that wouldn't make her look like either a petulant toddler who had been forced to leave her toys and come out to play with the big boys and girls, or just a plain old wimp. She cast her eyes around the clearing that housed the Ultimate Adventures office and shuddered when she saw the quad bikes and mountaineering gear through the open door of the on-site storeroom, a separate wooden structure at the back of the reception lodge.

The only sound in the woodland, apart from the melody of birdsong, was the persistent beat of her heart thumping through her eardrums and pumping adrenalin around her body. However, hadn't she felt exactly the same before she'd embarked on the field archery course Matt had introduced her to a couple of months ago and she had loved that!

'Had to keep Rosie in the dark about our final destination, but I think we're good to go.'

'Well, trust me, Rosie; you're in for a real treat! You'll love the obstacle course!'

'The obstacle course?'

She should have known it would be something like this, and whilst she was alarmed about making her debut on Matt's famous assault course, not to mention the certainty that she would end up covered from head-to-toe in mud, she was relieved that her approaching humiliation was going to take place on *terra firma* and not high up in the treetops. She decided to be grateful for small mercies – just looking up at the zip wire overhead gave her vertigo.

Rosie knew how much effort Matt had put into designing the Ultimate Adventures assault course when he'd stepped into his father's shoes after his death, and how proud he was of his achievement. It was the most popular activity at the outward-bound centre. So, she straightened her shoulders, raised her chin and inhaled a long revitalising breath; the woody aroma of crushed pine needles and mulched bark tickled at her nostrils and calmed her nerves a little. A least she wouldn't have an audience for her approaching mortification.

Matt disappeared into the storeroom and returned with their safety equipment. Under his careful instruction, she wriggled into the elbow and knees pads, pulled her helmet over her curls, and went to stand next to Grace and Josh to listen to Freddie's safety briefing – which Rosie knew was solely for her benefit. Every word caused a helix of alarm to wind its way ever tighter through her body, but she refused to let her fears beat her. She was determined to grab this chance to be brave, to make her father, and Matt, proud of her.

Fortunately, the weather gods' mood had improved and they were now smiling down on the group by sending shafts of diaphanous sunlight through the branches overhead causing shadows to dance on the forest floor. She gritted her teeth, mainly to stop them chattering, and plastered a smile on her face.

'Okay, Rosie, are you ready?' said Freddie, his eyes sympathetic when he saw her smile falter into doubt. 'Don't worry, I'll go first, with Grace and Josh next, and then it's your turn. Matt has volunteered to bring up the rear guard so he can be on hand to offer help if you need it. We've decided that as this is just for fun, we're not going to race against the clock, but instead everyone should collect their coloured disc at the end of every obstacle for the reason that will become clear at the end. Right, have fun!'

Freddie gave everyone a fist bump and led the group to the

first challenge – an assortment of sturdy wooden stepping stones protruding from what looked to Rosie like her father's compost heap and smelt almost exactly the same. She suspected that if she fell off before she got to the end, she'd been sucked into its depths like quicksand, never to be seen again.

With astonishing speed, her three friends dashed across the quagmire of leaves and mulch, their knees pumping like pistons as they navigated each trunk. Rosie gulped and tossed a nervous glance over her shoulder at Matt. He gave her a smile and a brief nod of encouragement, and she began her slow negotiation of the first obstacle, building up a momentum that helped her to get to the other side without incident.

A feeling of intense relief and accomplishment seeped into her veins and she turned around to beam at Matt until he indicated the next challenge and her stomach performed a somersault.

'What am I supposed to do here?'

She heard the wobble of trepidation in her voice as she contemplated what lay ahead. There was no sign of Freddie, Grace or Josh because they had forged on ahead, but also due to the towering pyramid of intertwined rope that was blocking her view.

'Climb up onto the platform, grab hold of the rope, and swing yourself over the water to the other side. Don't forget to grab onto the rope-netting when you land or you'll tumble into the trough – and trust me you don't want to do that – then climb to the top of the apex and down the other side. I'll be right behind you.'

Before she could formulate a persuasive argument in support

of a retreat back to the comfort and warmth of the lodge, Matt had urged her forward. She grasped her courage by the scruff of its neck, coming to the conclusion that it really didn't pay to think too carefully about what she was faced with, just to fling herself at whatever lay in front of her and hope for the best.

She grabbed the rope, pulled it taut and leapt from the platform, landing in an ungainly heap on the netting. She managed to scramble upright, but struggled to climb to the top, instantly regretted her agreement to let Matt take up the 'rear guard' because it meant he had a glorious view of her swinging behind. However, despite her palms smarting from the rub of the rope, when she reached the other side of the pyramid she felt on top of the world.

'Yay! I did it! I did it!'

Rosie pogoed on the spot clapping her hands just like Mia would have done, and the exhilaration of what she had achieved gave her the impetus to contemplate the next obstacle. However, before she stepped forward she remembered to jog over to the green wooden box at the side of the pathway that ran alongside the course to grab her yellow disc and store it in her pocket.

'Enjoy that?' asked Matt, sweeping elegantly to her side a few moments later.

'It was amazing!'

Their eyes met for a brief moment and Rosie struggled with the intensity of the emotions that swirled through her body. A sudden impulse to reach up and kiss Matt was almost too much to resist.

'On to the next challenge then.'

She followed the direction of Matt's finger to where a collection of gates, hedges, fences and wooden barrels were strategically placed for a challenge that looked to Rosie like a show jumping gymkhana, complete with the water ditch.

'Want me to go first?'

'Please.'

She watched Matt vault over the jumps like a seasoned Olympic athlete before grasping a parallel handrail of rope to help him balance as he strolled across a series of twelve wooden barrels that rotated with every step he took. Finally, he performed a flying leap over the ditch at the end.

'Your turn!'

She relegated her swirling nerves to the back of her mind and launched herself forward, clearing the hurdles without too much effort. However, when she stood on the barrels they rotated swiftly and she was tipped forward and fell flat on her face.

'You just have to go for it!'

She clutched at the ropes on either side of her, struggling to maintain her balance, then took Matt's advice. With a burst of confidence and a smile stretching her lips, she sprinted as fast as she could to the end, sending the barrels into a spin behind her as she leapt from each. Unfortunately, she was unable to slow down in time, lost her footing on the final barrel, and slammed into a puddle of sludge.

'Euwh! It's freezing!'

'Ready for the next one?' laughed Matt as Rosie collected her reward from the box.

'Of course!'

With every minute that passed, Rosie's confidence mounted. She ignored the fact that twigs and dry leaves nestled in her curls, that sweat trickled from her temples and her fringe stuck to her forehead beneath her helmet. Her palms were not only raw from the continuous friction, but blisters threatened too. Yet, she could feel the intensity of Matt's reassurance vibrate through the air which galvanised her to press on.

'Okay, so the next challenge is the maze. I know I said we weren't timing the course today, but if you're not on the other side in five minutes, I'll come and get you. The box containing the discs is at the centre. Ready? Go!'

Rosie dashed into the arboreal labyrinth, switching left and right as she plunged deeper into its heart. Shards of shredded bark flicked in her wake as her heart pounded with determination to complete the challenge before the time was up. She wanted to prove to Matt that she could do this without needing him to rescue her. For the first time since she had arrived at Ultimate Adventures, she was actually enjoying herself. She hadn't thought of the drama caused by Theo's accident once since she'd set foot in the woodland – and she realised that was precisely the point.

A few second later she reached the middle of the maze and collected her yellow disc from the chest, then swivelled round to find the exit to the tangle of trees before Matt had chance to seek her. She faced a dead-end only twice before emerging triumphant, her cheeks glowing with heat and pride.

'You're a natural!'

'I don't know about that,' Rosie laughed, trying to rub a splodge of mud from her sleeve. The dirt should have freaked her out, but there was a distinct absence of her hygiene pixies lurking in the woodland that day. The ember of anxiety that burned in her abdomen whenever she was faced with even a smidgeon of a germ was no longer an issue as she surged forward to the next challenge – one which under normal circumstances she would never contemplate attempting.

'You've probably seen this before,' said Matt, indicating a vast expanse of heavy rope mesh attached to the ground with wooden pegs beneath which she was expected to slither on her stomach. If she wasn't already covered in a coating of mud, dust, bark and leaves then she would be when she'd completed this challenge.

It was a lot harder than it looked and she was grateful for her protective clothing, especially her knee and elbow pads. When she emerged at the other side, her muscles were screaming in objection to the physical exertion that baking scones and cupcakes did not require. She was out of breath and craving a drink, but there was only one challenge remaining.

'Okay, I know this is the hardest bit, but I'll be right behind you.'

Matt escorted Rosie to a rope ladder dangling at the bottom of a tree as tall as a telegraph pole. She squinted into the treetops and groaned as she realised what the finale was going to entail. She could just about make out a wooden platform in the canopy overhead, along with a cat's cradle of steel cables and ropes. A twist of terror invaded her body and she gulped down her rising panic.

'Matt—'

'When you arrived here, did you think you would complete any of the obstacles?'

'Well, no, but—'

'So you'll ace this one too. Just one piece of advice – don't look down.'

Rosie stepped forward, panic ricocheting around her brain, all ancillary thoughts extinguished save for the trial ahead of her. She gritted her teeth, summoned up her courage and began her ascent towards the clouds. She counted every rung, focusing her attention on each one separately until, eventually, her throat dry and a cacophony of alarm pounding through her ears, she emerged onto the creaky platform.

Forgetting Matt's advice, she chanced a peek over the edge and was visited by a sharp nip of vertigo. She stepped back, hugging the tree's trunk to her spine as a bout of uncontrollable trembling gripped her.

Matt was at her side immediately, wrapping his arms around her, whispering calming words to ease her anxiety. His warm breath on her cheek and ear lobe caused spasms of desire to cascade through her body, and the fragrance of his citrusy cologne sent her senses into overdrive. Suddenly her trembling had nothing to do with the fear of being suspended so far from the ground. When she met Matt's eyes and saw the way he was looking at her, his mouth scarcely a centimetre from hers, her body ignited with heat. Whilst Freddie's safety briefing hadn't specifically banned kissing, perhaps they weren't standing in the best place to indulge in a passionate embrace.

Nevertheless, this was a day of firsts and without further

hesitation she leaned forward and pressed her lips against Matt's, gentle to start with, until her emotions overtook her sensible side and she revelled in the maelstrom of pleasure being so high up in the foliage paradise produced, not to mention the feel of Matt's muscular body pressed against hers.

When she eventually rejoined reality, she beamed at Matt, but before she could formulate the words to explain how she felt about reconnecting with him again, she heard cries from the woodland floor below. Freddie, Josh and Grace had clearly completed the course and arrived to offer her their support on the final challenge.

'You can do it, Rosie!'

'Don't look down!'

'Just look straight ahead!'

'Are you okay?' asked Matt his eyes scouring hers for an answer.

'Better than ever.'

And that was the truth. Whenever she was with Matt, she felt as though she could conquer the world. No challenge was too taxing, no decision too complex, no experience dull or boring. His presence in her life made her nerve endings zing, and not just when they were eleven metres from the ground. She understood what those feelings meant, and the realisation filled her with happiness.

As Matt helped her into the zip wire harness and attached the carabiners, every single one of Rosie's senses woke from their habitual slumber. Every nerve-ending tingled, every pore in her body exuded confidence and determination.

With a whoop of joy, she leapt from the treetop platform

into the air, unconcerned about the consequences. The flight carried her on an exhilarating journey, sending squirrels and blackbirds scuttling for cover, her copper hair flying in her wake from beneath her safety helmet, the whiff of damp earth floating on the breeze until she landed in an undignified heap on a mound of shredded bark at Freddie's feet.

'Awesome!' she cried as Matt landed next to her.

Rosie couldn't help herself. She was so overwhelmed with what she had achieved that she slung her arms around Matt's neck and hugged him in front of everyone, overjoyed when he responded by lifting her from the ground and swinging her round and round to cheers and whistles of approval from their audience.

'Thanks, Matt. That was the most amazing thing I've ever experienced and it was exactly what I needed. I feel like I can overcome any kind of challenge life throws in my direction now!'

'Didn't I tell you that you'd have fun? And it's great to see the real Rosie poking through that comfort blanket you're so determined to wrap yourself up in. You know my motto; life's short so you have to squeeze the most out of every day, push every boundary! It's what my dad always taught me to do; and it's why I built the assault course in the first place! Come on. There's one challenge remaining.'

Matt and Freddie lead the group to a set of eight wooden boards perched on easels in a clearing opposite the reception lodge – Rosie hadn't realised they had travelled round in a circle. The boards were colour-co-ordinated to match the discs that each contestant had collected, and presented a mental agility test, which, if completed correctly provided a key to a metal box underneath.

Rosie was in her element – having undertaken many similar puzzles with her father – and completed hers in minutes, whilst Josh struggled to slot his discs into the board in the correct order. She scooted to her box and removed a strange looking metal object which she held up, thinking it was a sort of trophy.

'Now it's all down to team work,' said Freddie, holding up his own cylindrical object. 'These are the components to a mechanical canon that will shoot a coloured flare into the air at random to indicate the final winner of the competition. Okay, go!'

By the process of trial and error, the team built the cannon and launched the flare.

'Yay! It's yellow! Rosie, you're the winner!' Grace flung her arms around Rosie as her face flooded with warmth and tears sparkled at her lashes. 'You were amazing! I had no idea you were a puzzle genius! I don't suppose you've also had a sudden flash of inspiration about who attacked Theo?'

Rosie shook her head as they made their way back to the store room to return their gear. 'No, but I'm keen to get back to asking questions!'

'Who's still on your list?' asked Josh, stretching up to store his helmet on the top shelf.

'We've spoken to Sam, Zara, and Penny, so we still need to talk to Theo, Abbi and Dylan.'

'Well, I doubt Theo set up his own accident, and I really don't want to think my bridesmaid or her boyfriend had anything to do with it either,' said Grace, shaking her head in resignation as they made their way back to where they had left their cars. 'Good luck, anyway.'

As Matt drove her back to the Windmill Café, Rosie had to agree with Grace. Maybe her earlier bout of confidence brought on by the kiss she had shared with Matt high in the treetops, had been misplaced.

Chapter 11

When they drew into the Windmill Café car park there was no sign of Mia or any of their guests, but Rosie knew they would all still be in the marquee putting the finishing touches to their trees. She was about to suggest they join them when her stomach growled its objection to her lack of consideration of breakfast. Also, she wasn't ready to say goodbye to Matt yet.

'Fancy brunch?'

'I'd love a coffee.'

Rosie prepared a cafétière of freshly ground coffee and a plate of pain aux raisin and set everything down on the table next to the French windows in the café. The weak December sunshine penetrated the glass with shards of golden light and a gentle breeze rustled through the leaves of the bay trees standing sentry on the threshold. The dawn chorus had moved on to the performance of a mid-morning concerto and if they hadn't had more pressing matters to discuss, that would have been the perfect time for her to talk to Matt. But time was running out and they had to concentrate on their objective of solving the mystery of Theo's accident.

'I'm convinced the reasons for Theo's accident must lie somewhere in his personal life,' mused Matt. 'Did you call your Uncle Martyn to ask for his help?'

'No, I thought we should talk to Theo first. But before we shoot over to the hospital, why don't we have a chat with Abbi and Dylan in case either of them saw anything in the woods that morning. That way we'll have a full picture to run past Theo.'

'Okay.'

'Who shall we start with?'

'Abbi, I think.'

'Why?'

'Because I've just seen her leave the marquee carrying a huge cardboard box back to the shepherd's hut. I'll go and ask her if she minds coming over to the café to talk to us.'

Matt swallowed down the last of his coffee, dumped his mug in the sink, and strode from the room. Rosie remained seated, wrestling with an irresistible urge to fill the sink with soapy water. She sat on her hands and started the counting exercises her sister had taught her, but it was no use. She couldn't ignore the clutter. She jumped up from the sofa, grabbed her Windmill Café apron and washed the crockery, dried it and returned each item to its rightful home. A surge of relief swept over her when the chore was complete and she relaxed, until she spotted a stray raisin on the bench. She grabbed the dishcloth and quickly swept away the debris just as Matt and Abbi appeared on the doorstep.

'Hi, Abbi. How's the Christmas tree decorating coming along?'

'Amazing! I love how it's coming together. It's a fabulous

way to showcase the variety of handbag designs on offer without the expense of creating each one in full-size – and I'm hoping that the quirkiness might score me and Dylan some extra points in the judging, too. But the best thing is that it's keeping my nerves over being chief bridesmaid at bay, not to mention being interviewed by the police about what happened to Theo. Oh, by the way, he's back.'

'Theo's back?'

Rosie shot a glance in Matt's direction. If they had known Theo had been discharged from hospital that morning, they would probably have decided to talk to him before Abbi.

'Yes, and guess where he is? Recuperating in his lodge? No, he's in the marquee, working on his festive masterpiece, complaining vociferously about the time he's lost and how the fact that his arm is in a sling will adversely affect his "work of art". But do you know what the worst thing is? He's insisted on erecting a screen around his tree so no one can see what he's doing! *And* would you believe that he point-blank refused to have breakfast with Penny to talk about what the police have said to him, even accused her of trying to sabotage his entry by wasting his time. He's a difficult man to like is Theo Morris. You know, if it wasn't for the effect all this is having on Grace, I'd be suggesting you ditch the sleuthing – Theo doesn't deserve your efforts. I bet you've not had time to work on your trees, have you?'

'True, but I think Mia has ours under control,' giggled Rosie.

Abbi plonked herself down on the overstuffed white leather settee, folded her ankles neatly and placed her laced fingers on her lap in the perfect ladylike pose. Rosie felt like an uncoordinated elephant when she sat next to her but she remembered that Abbi had spent three years at drama school preparing for the day her career would ascend to the dizzying heights she craved. She already looked like a star-in-waiting with her immaculately coiffed bob the colour of burnished gold, and flawless skin, her face so well made-up that it resembled a Pierrot's mask. But what really drew Rosie's eye was her gorgeous sunflower-yellow handbag that she'd discarded on the seat next to her. Grace's best friend really was a woman of many talents.

'So, what did you want to ask me?'

'Do you have any idea at all why someone would want to harm Theo?' asked Rosie.

'Apart from his condescending personality and insatiable desire to triumph over everyone else, you mean? No, none whatsoever.'

'When you were waiting for us to arrive back from our cycle ride on Wednesday morning, did you see anything at all? Anything out of the ordinary?'

'No, nothing. I was too busy wondering how Dylan was getting on with all you sports enthusiasts. That cycle *race* was the first time he'd ridden any real distance since his accident. All my attention was focussed on whether he would actually make it to the end. I did remind him that he could say "no", but he wanted to prove to himself that he'd conquered his fears and I think he did that amazingly!'

'So, there was no way Dylan would have considered taking a shortcut through the woodland.'

'Absolutely not!'

But Rosie had noticed a flicker of something behind Abbi's bright blue eyes and again she wanted to ask about what had happened to Dylan, but she decided to take a different tact to draw her out and loosen up the conversational flow.

'Congratulations on your role in the crime drama, by the way. It must be a dream come true for you!' Abbi's expression changed immediately and Rosie knew she had made the right decision, despite seeing Matt heave a sigh of frustration which she chose to ignore. 'What else have you been in?'

'Just a couple of walk-on parts, really. I've only been back from travelling for a few months so I'm still building up my CV. You might have seen me in *The Friends Fiasco*?'

Rosie shook her head.

'What about *A Carousel of Creations*?'

'No.'

'What about *Waiting for William*? You must have seen that?' Abbi's perfectly sculpted eyebrows raised even higher up her smooth forehead.

'Erm, possibly—'

'Well, I'm sure you go to the cinema. I haven't actually told anyone this yet, but I've just been offered a role in a David Bradshaw movie. Oh gosh, I'm so excited! I play a lawyer who lures the star – none other than Alex Appleby – into a deserted barber's shop in the back streets of Manchester. I think it's a romantic comedy. Anyway, I've been studying my lines for weeks because I need to be word perfect.'

'Sounds amazing,' smiled Rosie.

'It's not a huge part but I've been assured that it's pivotal to the plot. I need to be at the top of my game to make a good impression. Dylan isn't much good at helping me learn my lines though and I've got a really awful memory because of an illness I had when I was a child.'

'So how *do* you learn them?'

'I just have to go over them again and again. Unfortunately, when I'm nervous my mind tends to go blank.'

'I know just what you mean. I was exactly the same when I sat my exams at school.'

Rosie didn't want to explain to Abbi that the reason for her difficulties had nothing to do with a poor memory and everything to do with losing her father, and her mother falling to pieces to such an extent that they lost their home and had to move to a different part of the country and a different school.

'Me too. I was totally useless,' laughed Abbi. 'If it wasn't for my sister I'd never have got into drama school.'

'What do you mean?'

'Oh, just that Alicia was blessed with a photographic memory. It's so unfair because we're twins! What's even more galling is that she doesn't even use her God-given talent. She's a sculptor and spends all her time throwing blobs of clay at wooden boards and then painting them.'

Matt leaned forward and cleared his throat, reminding the women that he was still in the room.

'So,' said Rosie, hurriedly. 'I hope you don't mind, Abbi, but we've asked everyone this question. What did you and Dylan do on Tuesday night after having dinner at Zara and Sam's lodge?'

'We went back to our little shepherd's hut. Dylan wanted

to get a good night's sleep because he had to be up for the cycle ride at six.'

'And after he left? What did you do?'

'I went for a run, then I showered and joined the others to watch the end of the race.'

'Did you see anyone when you were out running?'

Abbi paused, crinkling her forehead as she scoured the crevices of her memory for any recollections of that fateful morning. 'No, I don't think so. I wasn't really taking much notice to be honest.'

'So, there's no one who can vouch for your whereabouts from the time Dylan left the hut until you arrived at Ultimate Adventures?'

'Erm, no, I don't suppose—Hey, I hope you're not suggesting I had anything to do with Theo's accident! He's a complete pain in the backside, always sticking his nose in other people's business, but I would never do anything like that! Why would I jeopardise my best friend's wedding?'

Again, Rosie noticed a flash of indecision behind Abbi's eyes.

'Is there something you're not telling us, Abbi? Matt and I are only trying to help Grace and Josh so that they can have the wedding they always dreamed of. If there is something, you should tell us.'

'Oh, it's nothing much really. A misunderstanding, that's all.'

Abbi selected a thick strand of hair and began to coil it around her index finger, struggling whether to divulge what was obviously on her mind.

'Abbi?'

'Oh, Theo was threatening to spoil everything,' she blurted out, averting her eyes to study her fuchsia-pink manicure.

'Spoil everything? What do you mean?'

Abbi inhaled a fortifying breath, clenched her jaw and looked Rosie in the eye with the confidence and poise of an Oscar-winning leading lady.

'Theo Morris is such a moron. Somehow – I don't know how – he found out that I'd been caught driving under the influence. No one was hurt or anything and I'm mortified about what I did – I don't know what came over me. I lost my licence of course, which is one of the reasons I decided to go travelling with Grace. I've learnt my lesson and I never drink a drop when I'm driving now. But David Bairstow, the director of this new film I'm in, is a teetotaller and one of the stipulations in our contracts is that everyone must abstain from alcohol, and any other substance, whilst the shoot is taking place. I'm not sure what would have happened if Theo had informed him about my conviction. I might have lost my part, I might not, but I didn't want to take the risk. I couldn't bear it!'

'But how did Theo know?'

'I have no idea. I don't scream about it from the rooftops, but I suspect it was probably from Sam. Dylan was all for confronting him, but I didn't want any unpleasantness so I told him to forget it. Anyway, Theo would probably have loved an excuse to report any incident to the police – and that would definitely have put a stop to Dylan's business before the banks even have chance to squeeze his last penny from him.'

'What kind of business is Dylan in?' asked Rosie, noticing the anxiety in Abbi's voice.

'Football, would you believe!'

'Football?'

'Junior football to be precise. Coaching talented youngsters in the art of dribbling and that sort of thing. He loves it and it's really given him a new lease of life after, well, after what happened.'

Rosie saw that Abbi's habitual brightness had diminished since she had joined them in the café and her heart gave a nip of sympathy. She was about to press Abbi on the details of Dylan's accident when Matt swiftly curtailed their conversation.

'Thanks for your honesty, Abbi.'

Abbi pushed herself up from the sofa and made her way to the door. 'Just find out who did this so we can get on with enjoying Grace and Josh's wedding, will you?'

Matt waited until the clickity-clack of Abbi's footsteps receded before turning to Rosie. 'Another person on our list with a motive and no alibi.'

'Maybe they all did it.'

'What do you mean?'

'Perhaps all five of the Windmill Café's guests were involved in setting Theo up for a fall. It's possible.'

Matt stared at her for a beat. 'From what we know about our victim so far it wouldn't surprise me in the slightest if his friends had formed an orderly queue to throttle the guy. This inquiry is turning into an absolute nightmare!'

Chapter 12

'Theo?'

'Oh, it's you Rosie. Make sure you pull the screen back into place, will you? We don't want to encourage prying eyes, do we? Actually, I'm glad you've decided to put in an appearance at last. I wanted to ask you what the competition rules are for engaging an assistant when one of the competitors has a disability?'

Theo waved his arm, encased in a sling, around in the air, grimacing slightly at the sudden movement. Despite his sojourn in the hospital, he seemed in surprisingly good spirits, his dark blue eyes filled with passion for the project he was working on. For the first time, Rosie noticed how muscular he was, taking in his broad shoulders and the firmness of his biceps and how he towered over her as he waited for her reply. Without realising it, she took a couple of steps backwards.

'I'm sure if you can find a willing helper that would be fine, but should you really be doing this after what you've been through? Maybe you should sit this one out? Haven't the doctors at the hospital told you to rest?'

'Ah, but that's what everyone wants me to do, isn't it? Eliminate the competition!'

'It's just a bit of fun, Theo.'

'Who says I'm not having fun? I'd rather be here creating a masterpiece of festive fabulousness than wallowing in a hospital bed being pawed by all and sundry. Look, Rosie, don't take this the wrong way, but why don't you go off and distract some of the other competitors? I've already lost a whole day and every minute counts when you're aiming for perfection.'

Rosie opened her mouth to object to his curt dismissal but before she could formulate the right words, Theo had paused in his task of attaching a tiny metal car to one of the lower branches.

'Oh, but perhaps you can help me with something before you disappear? Do you happen to know what the Rev's hobbies are? I did google him before I came down here but there's surprisingly little about him online, just the usual ecclesiastical stuff, nothing personal, no Facebook page or Instagram account.'

'Sorry, Theo, I have no idea what the Rev does in his spare time.'

A wriggle of disquiet wove its way through Rosie when she recalled something Abbi had said earlier about how Theo knew so much about everyone. Clearly he was a man who did his homework, however small and insignificant his encounters or contests were going to be. Why would he bother to go to such lengths as to investigate the judge's likes and dislikes for a Christmas tree decorating competition when the prize was a tiny silver trophy fashioned in the shape of a Windmill?

'Never mind. I think I've got this in the bag, anyway. Prepare to be stunned, Rosie! An unfortunate accident isn't going to stop me from pulling out all the stops to produce the most amazing spectacle Willerby has ever seen in the arena of Christmas Tree Decorating!

'Accident? You think what happened to you was an accident?'

'Well, of course I'm going to wait until the police have conducted their enquiries, but as I told them when they came to take my statement at the hospital, that wire has to have been a trap set up by a rather incompetent poacher to catch deer or foxes.'

'I don't think—'

'Of course, poaching is still a crime and I expect the police to throw the book at whoever did this to me when they arrest them. I'm also contemplating making a claim for damages for my injuries; that should be interesting.'

'So, correct me if I'm wrong, Theo,' said Matt who had appeared inside the enclave that Theo had built around his precious tree, his expression reflecting his dislike for the man in front of him brandishing a miniature E-Type Jaguar dangling from a thin silver chain. 'Are you really expecting us to believe that you didn't do a recce of the woods before the race on Wednesday morning?'

'A recce?'

'Yes, because how else would you have known about the path from the road to the finishing line unless you had explored every inch of the woodland looking for a shortcut that would knock a few minutes of your time?'

'I—well—'

To Theo's credit, Rosie saw his cheeks colour and guilt take up residence in his eyes.

'It's called preparation, Matt. Any self-respecting competitor makes sure they're familiar with the course layout before a race. I'm sure you would agree with me, after all, it's what your father was famous for, isn't it? His close attention to detail, making sure every single eventuality was catered for?'

Rosie inhaled a sharp breath and for a moment she thought Matt was going to lunge at Theo. She wouldn't have blamed him in the slightest, but she stepped between the two men and asked the question that was burning in her brain.

'Theo, if you did do a recce of the woodland and found the shortcut, I take it you didn't come across the wire that you are adamant is merely an old poaching trap that someone has forgotten to move?'

'No, of course I—oh—'

Theo flashed his eyes to Matt and then back to Rosie, a sliver of fear now appearing in their sapphire depths

'Do you have any idea who would want to force you off your bike? I think even you have to accept that if the wire had been even a few inches higher, your injuries could have been fatal.'

'Why would anyone want to target me? Everyone loves me! But I do take your point. I think I'll just give the police a call to see if they've made any progress. Excuse me, would you?'

Rosie watched Theo dash from the marquee then turned to Matt.

'I think I've just realised how Theo operates.'

'What do you mean?'

'Remember when Abbi said Theo knew about her driving ban? And Zara saying she was surprised he knew about her grandfather's Rolls? And what about Theo turning up in Dubai and just happening to find Sam in a compromising position?'

'Yes?'

'Well, I think Theo could have stumbled on some information that someone didn't want him to reveal and decided to make sure he didn't. If that's true, I think we're looking at something much more malicious than incapacitating Theo so that he ends up being presented with the wooden spoon at the judging on Saturday.'

'If you're right, then we need to take a leaf out of Theo's book ourselves. I'll do some digging into his background – see if anything comes up. It has to be something pretty serious to go to such lengths. I'll give your uncle a call to see if he has any suggestions about where we could start looking, then I might try to speak to DS Kirkham.'

'Okay, tell Uncle Martyn I said hi.'

Rosie smiled as Matt followed in Theo's footsteps out of the tent before turning her attention on the circle of magnificent fir trees in various stages of completion. The whole room zinged with jolly conversation, festive music and the enticing aroma of crushed pine needles with a top note of the cinnamon sticks that floated in the mulled wine. She was about to head for the refreshment table manned by Mia when her quest was interrupted by someone calling her name.

'Hey, Rosie? Come over here and tell me what you think!'

Rosie made her way to where Abbi was putting the final touches to her Christmas tree.

'Wow! Abbie, it's stunning – a real explosion of colour!'

Rosie feasted her eyes on what Abbi had created. Her tree was adorned with a kaleidoscope of brightly coloured leather goods; not only handbags, purses and key rings, but luggage labels, lipstick holders, mirror cases, everything a girl could want in the accessory arena fashioned from pinks, oranges, yellows, reds and whites. Garlands of silver and gold tassels completed the look which wouldn't have looked out of place in Selfridge's luggage department.

'Thanks, Rosie. Would you mind helping me to take a few photographs?'

'I don't mind at all, but I think Penny might be the best person to ask – it's her area of expertise, isn't it? Hang on, I'll go and ask her.'

Rosie spotted Penny crouching next to the tree furthest away from Theo's and made her way over.

'Oh my God! Penny, that's amazing! I love it, it's just so original!'

'I wanted to showcase the wildlife that make their home in trees such as the fir and the spruce,' explained Penny, pride radiating from her whole body, along with a blast of her signature patchouli oil. It was the first time Rosie had seen her in a colour other than black, taking in the jaunty

Christmas themed scarf she had used to tie her hair away from her face.

'You must have spent hours making all these decorations!'

Rosie took a tour around Penny's tree, marvelling at her creativity. Every branch held a tiny animal – red squirrel, hedgehog, dormouse, fox, badger, deer – all of which had been moulded from clay and painted with exquisite accuracy.

'What's this animal?'

'It's a pine marten, a bit like a weasel.'

'Oh, I love this robin! And is this a chaffinch?'

'No, actually, it's a chiffchaff! I love that name, don't you? And that's a woodpecker!'

'You are very talented, Penny. Speaking of which, would you mind taking a break to perform the role of star photographer? Abbi wants to use her tree in an advertising campaign for her new business.'

'I'd love to! I haven't had chance to check everyone's trees out yet, so that'll give me a great excuse to see what the competitions like. Apart from Theo's entry, of course. I see he's screened his off. You know, he's hardly said two words to me since he got back from the hospital. Anyone would think it was me who set up that tripwire!'

'I'm sorry, Penny.'

'Not your fault, Rosie.'

Penny collected her duffle bag and trotted off towards Abbi's tree, pausing occasionally to check out the other entries in the competition on the way.

'Hi Rosie. Will you tell Grace that she might have gone

just a little bit over the top with the decorations, please?' said Josh, rolling his eyes in amusement as Grace attached yet another silver horseshoe to the upper branches of her Christmas tree.

'Hey, a bride can never have too many baubles! Aren't these adorable, Rosie?'

Grace held out a pair of mini silver bells dangling from a pale ivory ribbon.

'They're gorgeous! And I love these engraved hearts!'

'When the judging is over, we're going to give them to our wedding guests as wedding favours. I adore everything on our tree but the *pièce de résistance* has to be the wedding angel, don't you think? Mum and I spent hours getting the outfit right.' Grace leaned forward to whisper in Rosie's ear. 'It's a perfect replica of my wedding dress and veil.'

Rosie heart ballooned with affection for Grace as she continued to unwrap a plethora of additional decorations, from fluffy white strands of glittering tinsel to pom-poms made from tulle, sixpences encased in silver photo frames, entwined wedding rings and gem-encrusted tiaras.

'Erm, Grace, what are these?'

Rosie fingered what looked like a paintbrush whose ends had been given an electric shock.

'Oh, I love those! They're what chimney sweeps use – they're supposed to be lucky. I'm not sure why,' she laughed as she climbed up to the top of the step ladder to add a spectacular wedding wreath made from white and silver baubles, ribbons and what looked to Rosie like holly leaves and berries that had been sprayed white.

'I really don't know where you and Carole found the time to do all this.'

'Everything is being reused on Sunday! This wreath will hang on the door of the church, these silver sixpences are being given to the children when Josh and I come through the kissing gate as husband and wife, those pom-poms have been infused with lavender and are destined for Josh's gran and great aunt, and these.' Grace handed Rosie a miniature bottle of champagne with a white label and silver foil neck. 'Will go down well, I'm sure.'

Rosie smiled at the bride-to-be whose eyes sparkled with anticipation for her special day and she experienced a blast of renewed determination to solve the mystery surrounding Theo's crash in the woodland. The last thing Grace and Josh deserved was for their wedding to be forever linked to a nasty accident involving one of their guests. If the culprit wasn't identified, the whole day would be overshadowed by rampant speculation when the rest of the guests arrived, and she would do anything to prevent that, including inviting everyone to lunch in the Windmill Café so she could encourage them to relax and maybe reveal something of interest.

Chapter 13

Despite Rosie asking everyone staying in the lodges to join her at the café, Sam, Theo, and Dylan had declined so they could continue working on their trees. As Matt has disappeared to make his calls and catch up on a mountain of paperwork at Ultimate Adventures, that left the women to enjoy a gossip.

'Do you think the police are any closer to making an arrest, Rosie?' asked Zara as she spooned fresh coffee into a large cafétière. 'I don't mind admitting that after everything that's happened this week, I'm really missing my boys – and so is Sam.'

'I'm not sure, but Matt's promised to give DS Kirkham a call this morning,' said Rosie, setting a huge pan of homemade minestrone soup down in the middle of the table around which everyone had congregated and handing out spoons and peppermint and white serviettes.

'Well, I wish they'd hurry up with their investigation,' muttered Mia as she lifted a rosemary-studded focaccia from the oven sending a mouth-watering aroma of warm baked bread into the café. 'It's really not fair that Theo's accident is the focus of everyone's attention instead of Grace and Josh's wedding – or our inaugural Christmas Carousel contest.'

Mia flung her tea towel onto the back of her chair in disgust, but her irritation didn't last long. Since the moment she'd stepped into the café to help Rosie prepare lunch, she had floated from one task to the next, humming along to the Christmas tunes she had blaring from the radio, beaming as she licked melted chocolate from her fingers, even performing a twirl as she scattered a handful of pasta into the soup pan. She looked like she was taking part in a culinary musical.

When Rosie questioned her sparkling mood, Mia divulged every detail of her date with Freddie the previous evening, declaring him to be the most handsome *and* the most interesting guy in the whole of Norfolk and that she couldn't wait to see him again. Then she had collapsed into a heap of giggles when she asked Rosie if she thought Freddie would mind if she asked him to wrap himself up in Christmas paper on Christmas morning.

'Oh, by the way Rosie, did I tell you that Dan Forrester from the Willerby Gazette called me yesterday to say he's coming over to the windmill tomorrow to take a few photographs and do a piece on the winning tree? When I contacted him in November to invite him to cover the contest, he said he was much too important to attend such *parochial* events. I reckon he's only changed his mind because of the police investigation and that's the angle he'll be playing up.'

Rosie sighed as she finished whipping up a huge bowl of mascarpone for the cranberry and white chocolate cheesecake she'd prepared for their dessert, then took a seat in between

Abbi and Mia before handing round the soup bowls and urging everyone to dig in.

'How's the investigation coming along, Rosie?' asked Penny, helping herself to a slice of the focaccia to dip in her minestrone. 'Any news?'

'Nothing, I'm afraid. We've spoken to everyone apart from Dylan. Theo' was adamant that it's an attempt at poaching gone wrong. He didn't think it's possible that anyone could have been targeting him.'

'Hey! Perhaps we could all get involved in a bit of sleuthing?' suggested Abbi, her eyes shining with enthusiasm. 'What clues have you found so far, Rosie? Tyres tracks in the woods? A discarded sweet wrapper next to the storeroom? Perhaps a letter written in code pinned to a tree?'

'None of the above. Maybe Theo is right and it was an animal trap.'

'I love all those murder mysteries on the TV,' mused Zara, as she swirled her spoon in her soup distractedly. 'There are always plenty of clues, but I can still never guess who the murderer is until the very end so I'd be totally useless in the role of PI Vardy.'

'Speak for yourself!' laughed Abbi. 'I think I'd look great in a deerstalker!'

Lunch was devoured with gusto and exuberant compliments were issued to Rosie and Mia, along with requests for the recipe for the cheesecake and the iced ginger biscuits that Mia had made and cut into Santa hat shapes. Rosie had just started on the clearing up when Sam appeared at the café's door.

'Is everything okay?' asked Zara, a flicker of concern in her tone at her husband's unexpected arrival.

'Everything's fine! Zara, will you stop fretting about the kids. Hasn't your mum told you they're having a ball? What with ice cream for breakfast, chocolate biscuits whenever they want them, and helping your dad build a treehouse in the garden – it's like a chapter from Swallows and Amazons! Tell you what, why don't I treat you to a trip to the coast? We'll go for a brisk walk along the sea front to blow away the cobwebs and finish up with a pint in the Drunken Duck.'

'Okay, you're on. But only after we've helped Rosie and Mia with the washing up.'

'Don't worry, we're fine,' Rosie assured her, secretly relieved that she would have her beloved café to herself so she could indulge in to a full-on session of cleaning without having to face the barrage of questions she was usually subjected to about her thoroughness. Explaining her obsession never got any easier.

'What about you, Penny? Fancy joining us?' asked Sam, clearly aware of the state of her relationship with Theo and offering her an alternative to spending the afternoon by herself.

'Actually, I'd love a trip to the coast. Can you hang on whilst I fetch my sketch pad?'

'Sure. What about you, Abbi?'

'You know what, I think I'll go over to the vicarage and help Grace finish off the wedding favours,' said Abbi, uncurling her legs from beneath her bottom and reaching for her coat.

'Why don't you join them?' Rosie asked Mia. 'You've worked like a Trojan today, what with single-handedly sorting out the café's entry for the Christmas tree competition, and helping me to prepare lunch, it's your turn to take a break.'

'You can't fool me, Rosie Barnes. You just want the place to yourself so you can get stuck in to a cleaning marathon, don't you?'

'No, I was just—'

'Sorry, I didn't mean to sound unkind. Actually, I think I'll pop over to Ultimate Adventures. I'm expecting my zip wire instructor certificate to arrive any day! I can't wait to lead my very first expedition through the tree tops. Want me to reserve you a place, Rosie?'

'Maybe in the audience! Send Freddie my love, won't you?' she grinned, her heart soaring at the love written across Mia's pretty face.

'Absolutely.'

As soon as Mia closed the French doors, silence expanded into all four corners of the café and Rosie exhaled a long sigh of relief. She removed her box of cleaning goodies from the cupboard under the sink and made a start on her cleaning ritual. For the first time that day, she relaxed, relishing the rhythmic workout that was better than any Zumba class. She was so absorbed in her spraying and scrubbing that she didn't hear the door open and jumped when she heard her name.

'Rosie?'

'Oh, hi Dylan.'

'I don't suppose you could rustle me up a sandwich, could you? I'm starving and there's nothing but a few stale bread rolls in our lodge. Oh, and is that cheesecake?'

'Come in. Come in. How about a bowl of home-made minestrone and a slice of focaccia?'

'Wow, that sounds amazing! Thanks, Rosie.'

Dylan ate every scrap she put in front of him while giving her a running commentary on the current state of the Christmas trees in the marquee and his opinion on those that were in the running for the silver trophy and those worthy of the wooden spoon.

'Theo's driving everyone insane, as usual. I think I'll give him a wide berth this afternoon and take a walk up to the Drunken Duck.'

'Oh, if you give me a minute to grab my coat, I'll walk over there with you.'

Dylan's jaw opened in surprise, but he was far too polite to refuse. They made their way from the café and sauntered through the holiday site towards the road leading to Willerby. The December afternoon was blustery and fresh, the wind lifting Rosie's wayward curls high above her head and slapping them across her face with alacrity.

'Abbi said you used to be a medic?'

They had paused at a large, recently-excavated pond behind the peppermint-and-white shepherd's hut where Dylan was staying with Abbi. The fishpond was Graham's current work-in-progress where he planned to house a school of Koi carp. Water lilies and pond weed floated like mermaid's hair just beneath the surface and a solitary magpie hovered nearby.

'Yes, I was – until I had my accident.'

Rosie's ears pricked up. Maybe this was her chance to find out what had happened. She glanced at Dylan from beneath her eyelashes, unsure whether she should persuade him to excavate painful memories. Thankfully she didn't have to.

'I fell off my bike during a road race around Cornwall and fractured several vertebrae in my neck. At one point my surgeon wasn't sure whether I'd walk again let alone get back in the saddle. But I did. After everything that happened, and the gruelling physio to get me back on my feet again, I realised I wasn't getting any younger and it was time to shoot for my dreams. My parents were great, they helped me make one of the hardest decisions of my life – to give up my medical career in favour of fulfilling one of my long-held ambitions.'

Rosie's heart bounced when she saw the emotion on Dylan's handsome face.

'I handed in my notice and Dad was on hand to help me to set up my junior football academy. He's always been a sports fanatic, an avid Manchester United supporter, and he's definitely passed his passion on to me.'

'Did he play football when he was young?'

'Yes. He played for a local youth team, but it wasn't just football that fired his canons. He loved golf, cricket, archery, tennis – you name it. And do you know what? I do too. Oh, I know what I do now doesn't save lives, and some of my so-called friends have accused me of wasting my education, even accused me of taking up a place at med school that could have gone to someone more committed. But I'm much happier now than I've ever been. I've found my niche in the world at last and that feels great.'

'What does Abbi think about the academy?'

'She's really supportive, apart from the financial worries.

She's right, of course – the business is permanently strapped for cash. There's so much to think about on the management side of things, too. All I want to do is teach the kids to play a decent game of football. I hate all the admin stuff, the interminable paperwork, the negotiations with the insurance guys, the health and safety courses. I know it's important, but it takes up so much time. Dad used to do all that before he passed away.'

'Oh, Dylan, I'm really sorry to hear that,' said Rosie, warming to Dylan with every passing minute of their conversation. It took tremendous guts to give up a lucrative profession that you had studied hard for in order to follow your passion, and, of course, she understood the impact of losing a much-loved parent.

'Without Dad keeping on top of everything I really started to get into a mess.'

A shadow of sadness settled in Dylan's eyes and he slowed his walking pace.

'Football isn't just a sport, you know; a quick kick-around once a week. It's a means of getting young people outdoors, to exercise and socialise with people they may not otherwise have the chance to meet. Handled right, it can teach them discipline, and a good fast game can get rid of the excess energy that kids always seem to have in abundance. It also gives them a goal, to coin a phrase. I've come across lots of children whose parents couldn't care less if their children spend twelve hours a day, or more, in front of a computer screen, eating pizza, drinking soda. Some of them are actually very talented when they get to the academy and put the work in.

'But when I speak to their parents about their own part of the commitment needed to nurture their kid's talent; the early morning starts to drive them to an away game, the cost of the kit, never mind the academy's fees, well, they back off pretty quickly. There was one young lad last season, Cameron, he had great potential and he really loved his football, but his mum lost her job half way through the season and couldn't afford to send him anymore. The boy was heartbroken so I called round to their house and had a chat to his mum about helping out with laundering the club's kit and we managed to sort it out. Worked for me, worked for Cameron, and for his mum. He's now got a place at United's junior academy! It's one of my proudest achievements.

'But helping the kids out means there's less money in the academy's coffers. And what with subsidising the cost of the petrol for our away matches, buying the kids bottled water for when they forget to bring their own, never mind paying the club's rent and insurance—well—needless to say we're broke. I think we might have to close the doors in the new year.'

Rosie could see that the stress Dylan was under weighed heavily on his shoulders.

'Is there nothing else you can do? What about asking for a bank loan?'

'Already done that.'

Dylan averted his eyes as he began to chew at the skin on the side of his thumb nail.

'And I take it the answer was no?'

Dylan nodded. He turned his back on Rosie in a futile

attempt to hide his misery as he contemplated a future without his beloved academy. Fortunately, they had arrived outside Adriano's Deli and the waft of freshly baked pizza and roast coffee beans was irresistible.

'Fancy a coffee?' asked Rosie.

'I thought you'd never ask!'

Chapter 14

Rosie pushed open the cheery scarlet door to the deli, smiling at the familiar tinkle of the brass bell. The low hum of chatter mingled with a backing track of operatic music and the delicious aroma of rich espresso and warm pastries – Adriano's was a little slice of Italian heaven transported to the Norfolk countryside. The room had been decorated with an abundance of festive white fairy lights and a large Christmas tree stood in the corner festooned with miniature football scarves and rosettes in the colours of Adriano's favourite team – AC Milan. She considered asking him if he planned on entering it in the Windmill Café's Christmas tree competition. It was certainly original!

Rosie smiled at Corinne who was busy serving another customer but indicated the table next to the window. She wriggled out of her coat and stuffed her bobble hat in the pocket before meeting Dylan's eyes. She had been intending to use their time together to ask him about Theo's accident, to see whether there was anything he could add to what she and Matt had already uncovered, but after hearing about his financial woes, she was reticent about introducing yet another distressing thread to their conversation. She decided to go to the counter to order their coffees to allow Dylan a few moments of privacy to gather his thoughts.

'Hi Corinne. I fancy a bit of a treat this afternoon, but it all looks so amazing, it's hard to choose! What do you recommend?'

'Well, Adriano made one of his signature *torta della Nonna* this morning. He says it's an old family recipe and refuses to share it with even his most loyal employees! Fancy a slice of that?'

'Absolutely!'

'*Ciao*, Rosie!' cried Adriano, appearing from the kitchen with a platter piled high with cannoli. He set the pyramid of pastries down on the counter so he could envelope Rosie in a fragrant bear hug. She rolled her eyes at Corinne over his shoulder and saw her giggle. Adriano often greeted his customers effusively, it was part of the deli's charms. 'Ah, yes, you have made an excellent choice! As a fellow connoisseur, you must tell me what you think of my grandmother's pie! Here, take a piece for your friend, too. Looks like he could do with some cheering up!'

Rosie carried two huge slices of Adriano's *torta della Nonna* back to the table. When Dylan's eyes fell on the unexpected offering, his face lit up like the Christmas tree in the corner and he grabbed a fork and dug in with relish.

'Sorry, Rosie. My emotions seem to be getting the better of me at the moment. Abbi's totally consumed by the wedding and her next acting role, not to mention her new business enterprise, and I don't want to spoil things for her by moaning about what's going on with the academy. We'll manage, but I'm exhausted from trying to put a brave face on everything after the shock of losing Dad, supporting Mum, then the business worries, and now Theo's accident. The only bright star of the last two years has been meeting Abbi.'

Almost as if he'd wished it, the door of the deli burst open and Grace and Abbi tumbled in to join them. From that moment on their conversation took on a much more upbeat vibe, with the wedding arrangements being the focus of attention. Corinne delivered hot chocolates all round, and a sharing platter of Adriano's *cartocci* filled with brandy cream which were demolished in minutes.

'I don't want to put you and Matt under any pressure or anything, Rosie, but do you have *any* ideas about who might be responsible for Theo's accident yet?' asked Grace, her face creasing in desperation as she licked the last of the cream from her fingers. 'Even Mum's started to talk about cancelling the wedding, saying that tomorrow is our last chance to ring everyone before they set off. I think she might be right. Josh and I don't want to get married with a dark cloud of fear floating over the whole ceremony! So, if you could identify the person responsible by say, ten o'clock this evening, Josh and I will be eternally grateful?'

Rosie knew Grace was joking but she couldn't fail to see the hope in her eyes. She also noticed that both Adriano and Corinne had paused in their task of washing down the vacated tables to listen to her answer. A ripple of remorse wove through her body. Grace and Josh had put their trust in her and Matt.

Whilst she had no idea how Matt was getting on with his

investigations into Theo's background, she just couldn't bear to admit the truth that they were no closer to discovering the identity of the culprit than when they'd started; that everyone she and Matt had spoken to so far seemed to have a reason for wanting Theo to suffer, not to mention the opportunity to rig up the trap in the woodland. So, for reasons known only to her subconscious, she decided to embroider her reply with a splash of positivity.

'Actually, Matt and I might have some news shortly. We still have some loose ends to check first, though, so do you think you could keep this to yourselves? Just until we've told the police about what we've uncovered? We don't want the person responsible to be tipped off now that we have them in our sights, do we?'

'Oh, my God, you've no idea how happy I am to hear you say that! Thank you. Thank you. Thank you! Come on Abbi, let's get back and tell Mum, and finish those wedding favours!' Grace jumped from her seat to drag Rosie into a hug, but in her enthusiasm bounced straight into Corinne who had come to replenish Dylan's coffee. 'Ooomph! Sorry, Corinne, sorry!'

As soon as the door swung closed behind Grace and Abbi, a sharp twinge of guilt invaded Rosie's chest. What had she done that for? But she had only wanted to put Grace's mind at ease about the wedding. So, now it was even more crucial that she talked to Dylan about his recollections of the cycle ride. She would have preferred Matt to be with her to ask the questions that didn't occur to her, but she channelled her inner Miss Marple and launched in.

'Dylan, Matt and I have spoken to everyone staying at the

lodges, except for you. Would you mind if I asked you a few questions, just so we can get a complete picture?'

'What sort of questions?'

'Well, like, how well did you know Theo before the stag party?'

Dylan stared at Rosie with his soft hazel eyes, clearly fighting an internal battle whether or not to confide in her. When he eventually spoke, it was with a passion that shocked her.

'Well enough to loathe the guy.'

'What do you mean? Why didn't you like him?'

'When I said I was devastated about the demise of the academy, it wasn't about me, you know; it was about the kids whose parents don't give a damn. It's them I'm worried about. There's no one else stupid enough to give them lessons for free. I've sourced second-hand boots for them, organised lifts, arranged for Cameron's mum to wash their kit. You should see their faces, Rosie, when they turn out on the pitch with a clean strip and a pair of decent football boots, eager to spend a couple of hours kicking a ball around. What are they going to do now? God, I hate Theo!'

'What's Theo got to do with your football academy?' asked Rosie wrinkling her nose in confusion.

'I suppose it'll all come out when the police eventually get around to interviewing us all, and to be honest, I'm surprised Abbi hasn't told you already. At the beginning of this season, a couple of months after Dad died, I needed to pay the annual rent for our pitch and the use of the changing facilities. I didn't have the cash up-front before the kids' parents paid the fees but we had a big fundraising event coming up later on in September so I asked Theo if he could loan me the cash and I'd pay him back when we'd collected the funds.

'He hummed and haaed and gave me a lecture on fiscal responsibility, but he eventually agreed. Unfortunately, the charity fundraiser got cancelled because of a waterlogged pitch so I had to renege on my promise and I asked him to give me a bit more time. He said he needed the money himself as he'd seen an MG he wanted to add to his collection, but he *did* give me an extra month to come up with the money. I sold some of Dad's football memorabilia – a ball signed by the Man United squad when they won the treble, a strip signed by David Beckham, a few old programmes. It was a huge wrench to see the stuff go but I managed to raise the cash and pay Theo back in full.'

'So, what's the problem?' Rosie guessed there was more to the story.

'He asked for interest on the loan – almost another hundred pounds. I didn't have anything left to sell.'

Rosie wasn't surprised to see Dylan's fingers tremble as he reached up to brush his hair from his eyes. Her heart gave a stab of empathy for the handsome football coach with a heart of gold, so concerned with helping the youngsters in his community that he had overlooked his own financial well-being. And what was it all for?

The silence between them expanded and she decided it was time to share some of her own history with Dylan.

'You know, I do understand how you feel. I lost my dad when I was a teenager – heart attack brought on by the immense work pressure he was under. Mum couldn't cope; she forgot to pay the mortgage so our house was repossessed and we had to relocate to a new town which meant my sister and I had to change schools. I'd dreamed of going to university, of training to be a solicitor like my dad, but the grief and upheaval had an effect on my studies so studying for a degree wasn't an option.'

'I'm sorry, Rosie. Sometimes we're so wrapped up in our own problems we forget that others are struggling on in silence. It's just you seem so happy at the Windmill Café that I thought you'd been there for years.'

'Six months! You're right, though. I am happy here, but the journey to Willerby was by no means an easy ride! What I'm trying to say is, it's hard to move on, to start again. And it's tempting to cloak yourself in misery and blame every setback and mistake on your misfortune. I was with my ex, Harry, for two years before I discovered him rolling amongst the daisies in our little flower shop in Pimlico with one of our customers who had come in to finalise her bridal flowers.'

'I'm sorry to hear that, Rosie. The guy must be crazy, if you ask me. So how did you end up in Norfolk? And managing a café must be a shock to the system after qualifying as a florist.'

'Actually, when I realised I wouldn't get the grades to go to law school, I put all my effort into my back-up plan – a career in the food industry. I loved the Windmill Café as soon as I set eyes on it, and it had the added attraction of having a cute little studio upstairs. Perfect!'

'Would you ever go back to London? Or to floristry?'

Rosie knew that Dylan had no idea about Harry's proposal, but the simple questions he'd asked served to solidify her decision because she was able to answer his question without hesitation or regret.

'No. I love my life here, and the people in it. I'm staying in Norfolk, at the little Windmill Café. I still have dreams to pursue, though, and I intend to make a start on them as soon as I can.'

And she couldn't wait. She resolved to call Harry that night and explain that she was grateful for his generous offer of a business partnership, but that she would not be returning to Pimlico any time soon, if ever. Okay, her job at the café and her home in the windmill were by no means secure, but she was happy where she was and that was all that mattered.

However, it was much more than that – she had a plan for her future and she was excited about going back to college. In fact, perhaps she would send Harry an email instead, just so she could set out her reasons in black-and-white without him interrupting her or trying to persuade her that she had made the wrong choice which was what he had done when he'd visited her at the café at the beginning of December. She would be firm, explain her decision was non-negotiable and would ask him not to contact her again. She had to move on, like she'd been doing before his surprise reappearance at the Autumn Leaves Hallowe'en party.

She smiled to herself when she thought of what her sister Georgina would say. Whooppee!

'Thanks, Dylan. Talking to you has really helped me to put

a few things into perspective. Actually, whilst we're here, do you think I could ask you about the cycle ride?'

'I didn't have anything to do with Theo's accident, if that's what you think. Oh, I'm not saying something similar doesn't cross my mind when I lie awake at night, anxiety gnawing away at my gut. I might not be a doctor anymore but the basic oath we all take to do no harm will stay with me for ever.'

'Did you see anything suspicious when you were racing through the woods towards the finishing line?'

'Racing might be a bit strong where I'm concerned, but no, nothing I'm afraid. I hated taking part in that race, only did it for Josh. I'm much better on my own two feet with a football between them than I am on two wheels. It was a forgone conclusion that I would be bringing up the rear so I kept to the main roads all the way, unlike Theo who we know took the shortcut – and that was despite being a total stickler for the rules! But I didn't see anything. I wish I had.'

'What about the night before your ride?'

'Abbi and I had dinner with Sam and Zara, and Theo and Penny. We left early so I could get some sleep for the early start. And before you ask, I didn't see anything on my way over to meet everyone the next morning either. Sorry I can't be any more help.'

'You've been a great help.'

'Rosie, I'm so pleased we got to spend this time together. It's been good to talk, not to mention indulge in all these delicious goodies, but it looks like Adriano wants to close the deli and it's getting dark outside. I think the guys will be back from their walk along the coast by now, too. Come on, let's head over to the Drunken Duck. I could murder a pint.'

'Lead the way. Oh, hang on, that's my phone!'

Rosie waved goodbye to Adriano as he closed the door behind her and flipped the sign to Closed. She withdrew her mobile to check the message that had pinging into her inbox.

'It's a text from Grace. She and Abbi want me to help them gather a final few bunches of holly for the church on Sunday. You go on ahead, Dylan. I'll catch up with you later.'

'Okay, if you're sure?'

She nodded and waited until Dylan's retreating figure had disappeared into the pub on the other side of the village green before scrolling through her other texts. When she read Matt's message, a surge of relief rushed through her body. Could it be possible that what he'd discovered meant she hadn't been lying to Grace and Abbi after all? There were no details, but his archaeology into Theo's background had apparently excavated some interested information which he said he'd share with her over one of his famous curries if she was free for dinner that night.

Rosie's heart soared. It would be the perfect opportunity to talk to Matt, to tell him about her decision to stay in Willerby, but also to explain her reasons – that she couldn't bear the prospect of not seeing him again and telling him why, not with words, but with actions. She slotted her phone into the pocket of her jeans, dragged her knitted hat down over her curls and with a spring in her step she headed to her rendezvous with a holly bush.

Chapter 15

Perspiration prickled at Rosie's forehead as she jogged towards the large wooden cabin that housed the offices of Ultimate Adventures where Grace had asked her to meet them. Beyond the leafy canopy overhead, dusk was in its last throes sending ribbons of violet and salmon through the wide expanse of dark turquoise sky. Unsurprisingly, the air held a definite nip, but the evening was mild for December.

Her mind whirled in anticipation of meeting Matt later and, over an intimate dinner at his home, finding out what he had discovered to make him so excited. She also rehearsed in her head what she was going to say about her decision to stay and about her feelings for him. This was going to be the fastest holly gathering expedition she'd ever attended, but she knew Grace and Abbi would understand.

She stomped up the steps to the veranda and the safety light switched on, but there was no sign of anyone. Disconcerted, she fished around in her pocket to check Grace's message again.

You are cordially invited to attend a holly and mistletoe scavenger hunt with me and Abbi! Mum needs more floral decorations for the church and we need your expert eye! Meet you at Ultimate Adventures in ten minutes. Grace xx

She checked her watch. 5 o'clock. Okay, so it had taken her fifteen minutes to get there on foot, but surely, they would have waited for her? Ergh! She wished she was with Dylan in the Drunken Duck, enjoying a glass of red wine before driving over to Matt's. She squinted through the trees into the darkness.

'Grace? Abbi? It's Rosie.'

Shielding her eyes, she peered through the window of the lodge, but, of course, there were no lights on inside. The whole place was deserted apart from the woodland inhabitants who cast accusatory eyes over her interruption of their nocturnal leisure time. She wrinkled her forehead in confusion. Perhaps Grace had sent her text before setting off from the vicarage?

Oh well, she thought, maybe they'd been held up. She keyed in Grace's number and was surprised to see there was no signal so decided to retrace her steps. She hopped down the veranda steps and as she made her way back towards the driveway, she noticed the door of the storeroom at the back of the cabin was ajar and she relaxed.

Separate from the lodge, this was where Matt and Freddie housed all Ultimate Adventures' equipment; the climbing gear, the safety harnesses and helmets for the zip wire, spare clothing for those who turned up ill-prepared. Inside was a cornucopia of tools and gadgets that would cause any kind of extreme sports enthusiast to glow green with envy.

She walked towards the lock-up, her boots crunching on

the gravel as she went. The last gasp of daylight trickled through the branches and her stomach gave a surprise flip of concern. She hadn't thought to bring a torch with her.

'Grace? Abbi? It's me! Are you in here?'

There was no reply.

'Grace?'

Silence.

Rosie gulped down her anxiety. What if Grace and Abbi had been searching for torches and Theo's assailant had found them? Could they be lying in a pool of blood, unconscious, on the storeroom floor?

Without considering the risks, she yanked the door open and rushed inside. She paused, taking a few moments for her eyes to adjust to the gloom before scouring the area. A whoosh of relief flooded through her veins when no terrible scene met her eyes. She could hear a scraping sound coming from the bathroom-cum-changing cubicle at the back of the room and made her way towards the door.

'Grace?'

She tentatively reached into the windowless room and pulled on the light switch but the cubicle was empty. Someone had left the extractor fan on and a whirling grating noise filled her ears. A wriggle of fear crept down her spine and her heart performed the backing track to the drama by hammering out a concerto of unease against her ribcage. She switched off the fan, extinguished the light, and retraced her steps to the entrance.

Just as complete panic was about to set in, she heard the familiar buzz of a quad bike engine bouncing through the tangle of shrubs behind the storeroom. She forced her face into a mask of nonchalance, and waited on the threshold with a confident smile, but the engine was cut before the bike appeared. She rolled her eyes and trudged round to the back of the shed.

'I thought you weren't coming!'

Clad in black leather from head to toe and wearing a full safety helmet, the rider dismounted and turned to face her. Before Rosie had chance to wonder why Grace still had the visor down, she was ceased her by the shoulders and spun around, her wrists yanked behind her back and secured with a plastic tie.

'What the hell?'

Terror zapped through her body as an arm hooked around her throat and she was urged forward, back into the storeroom and towards the bathroom at the rear.

'What's going on? Who are you? What do you want?' She tried to struggle but the anonymous rider was too strong.

'Let me go! Let me go!'

She managed to stamp down on her assailant's foot causing a sudden expulsion of air. For her trouble, a sheet of gaffer tape was slapped over her mouth and she was shoved to the ground head first. Pain ricocheted through her chin, the first part of her body to connect with the wooden floor. She was then dragged unceremoniously into the bathroom and the door was closed and padlocked.

Darkness pressed against her eyeballs, save for a tiny strip of light beneath the four-inch gap at the bottom of the door. She scrambled to her feet and began to kick at the door, but, like everything Matt and Freddie had a hand in, it was strong and sturdy and barely moved. When she paused in her assault, she heard the sound of tape being applied to the crack.

What the hell was going on?

Oh my God, she thought, why is the door is being sealed off with gaffer tape? What good would that do? The quad bike rider must be crazy if they thought that would do anything to hold the door.

With her heart flaying her chest, she listened to the retreat of footsteps and the sound of the outer door being slammed shut. A key turned in the lock, then, a few moments later, she heard the cough of the quad bike engine being coaxed back to life. She waited, all her senses on high alert, but the roar did not diminish as the rider sped off into the night as she had expected. Instead, the noise became louder until it was next to the wall where she was imprisoned.

She hadn't realised that tears were streaming down her face and every nerve ending sparkled with alarm. Using her knees, she located the toilet seat and sat down. Her heart was crashing so haphazardly that when the extractor fan fell from its housing she almost had a coronary. She screamed, launched herself to the right and knocked her elbow on the cistern, sending a splice of agony reverberating up to her shoulder.

Ignoring the pain, she felt around the room for the light pull. Finding it, she grasped it between her chin and her chest and pulled. It took a couple of attempts, but eventually she managed to light up the room. She twisted around to see a gaping hole in the wall, about five inches in diameter, where the extract fan had once been.

What the...?

It wasn't long before her part-formed question was answered in the most horrific of ways. A wide grey rubber tube, akin to a tumble dryer hose, had been inserted into the aperture and a spurt of white foam sealant applied to the outer circumference.

Rosie began to scream, but because of the tape she could only produce a muffled moan. She climbed onto the toilet seat and stared through the tube. There was nothing to see. A few seconds later, the quad bike engine became more insistent as the rider revved the accelerator, and the toxic stench of exhaust fumes spurted into the room. Nausea grasped at the back of Rosie's throat but she wasn't sure whether it was the fumes or her abject horror at what was happening that had caused it. She began to cough as the harsh acidic tang scorched her lungs.

She knew that if she vomited she would choke to death well before the oxygen had disappeared. She had to think quickly. She lay down on the floor, forced her tongue firmly into her cheek, and dragged her mouth along the floorboards until the tape began to roll and she was able to discard the gag. Once free, she mistakenly inhaled a few deep breaths and regretted her folly immediately as another intense coughing fit wracked her body.

A few moments later, the insistent revving ceased and morphed into a low, steady purr. Her kidnapper had clearly dismounted and made a run for it, leaving Rosie in the hands of the director of her fate.

She glanced around the room and her eyes fell on the toilet

roll. Turning her back and using her hands as a lever, she managed to unhook it from the holder. She jumped onto the toilet seat and raised her arms behind her back as high as they would go but, without forcing them out of joint, she couldn't reach the aperture. She unravelled the tissue and tried to secure it around her mouth and nose but it made no difference. Her head was starting to feel fuzzy and she knew she only had a few moments to come up with something, anything, that might save her life.

She dropped the toilet roll on the floor and, picking it up with her teeth, she climbed back onto the seat, stood on her tip-toes and launched herself forward towards the end of the tube. She missed, but only by a couple of inches. She repeated the action, getting a little nearer each time, and on her fifth attempt managed to plug the loo-roll into the opening. It wasn't a perfect fit but the fumes lessened considerably.

She cast her eyes around the room again, looking for something else that would help to keep her alive. She had an idea. She raised her foot and kicked the empty loo roll holder from the wall, then slotted the metal hanger under the door and dragged it backwards and forwards to remove the gaffer tape that had been hurriedly applied – now she understood why. The crack wasn't very wide but she prayed it would be enough. She lay on the floor and stuck her nose and mouth into the gap and inhaled.

The last thing to float through her mind as she succumbed to a dark, all-consuming oblivion was an image of herself, standing next to Matt in a charcoal morning suit and pink cravat in St Andrew's Parish church. He was one of the most intuitive people she had ever had the good fortune to meet. She sent up a fervent prayer that his exceptional intuition was on duty that evening.

Chapter 16

'Where on earth is Rosie? I've called her mobile and left a couple of voicemails. It's weird that she hasn't got back to me,' said Matt, screwing up his nose in concern.

'She's probably over at the vicarage with Grace and Abbi practicing her make-up for the wedding, or making a few more bouquets for the church, or even baking another batch of wedding cupcakes.' Freddie rolled his eyes at the craziness of it all.

'But she promised to meet me here for a drink an hour ago. I offered to cook her one of my famous curries so we could talk about our investigation before going to the police with what I found out this afternoon.'

'Well, there's your answer!' laughed Archie who had been listening to their exchange whilst changing one of the beer pumps. 'How can anything you throw together possibly match up to Rosie's cooking? The food at the Windmill Café is amazing.'

'Hey, I make an excellent chicken madras!'

'Perhaps Freddie is right – Rosie just popped in to see Grace first, forgot what time it was and is running late.'

Matt checked his watch and sighed. If it had been anyone other than Rosie they were talking about, he could have accepted Archie's explanation. However, Rosie Barnes was never late for anything. It was one of her most endearing traits. She had told him more than once that, in her view, people who were habitually late clearly assumed their time was more important than their friends' and that wasn't on. And anyway, that didn't account for why she wasn't replying to his texts or his calls and he had to admit he was worried.

With a flare of realisation, he understood how much he had come to enjoy being with Rosie, not just searching for clues and solving mysteries, but learning to understand her as a person and loving what he saw. If she *was* with Grace, gossiping over a glass of her beloved French wine then that was her prerogative; after all, she deserved an evening of fun, instead of panicking about the smooth running of the Christmas Carousel competition or raking over the intricacies of their investigation, but what did that mean? Had she rejected his invitation because she feared spending some time alone with him? Or had she decided to go back to London and didn't want to tell him.

He finished his beer and decided to return home to work through the information he'd unearthed that afternoon, slotting each snippet into the theory he knew was the right one. He had wanted to share his discovery with Rosie before going to the police, but perhaps he shouldn't wait any longer. The sooner an arrest was made the better.

'I'm off home, Freddie. Got lots to do. If Rosie does show up, can you tell her there's no problem about tonight? I'll catch up with her tomorrow.'

'Sure,' smiled Freddie with a touch of sympathy in his eyes.

'Hey, Matt. Hey, Freddie. Mind if I join you for a pint?'

'What can I get you, Dylan?' asked Archie.

'Guinness, please, and whatever you're having.' Dylan slumped down on the stool next to Freddie, placing his elbow on the bar and cupping his chin with his palm in a dejected fashion. 'No Rosie? Thought I might see her in here.'

'What made you think that?'

'Oh, we had coffee and a bit of a chat at Adriano's Deli this afternoon. We were on our way over to meet everyone in the Drunken Duck when she stopped to take a call, or it could have been a text, I suppose, and she said she'd catch me up.'

Matt opened his mouth to say something, but the mule's kick to his solar plexus caused the breath to become trapped in his throat. Thankfully, Freddie's response wasn't so lethargic.

'What time was this?'

'About an hour ago. I was going to come straight over here, but I bumped into Josh in the car park outside and he wanted a bit of a moan about all the wedding fiasco.'

'An hour ago?'

'Yes. Why? Where *is* Rosie?'

'Hang on.'

Matt grabbed his phone and called the vicarage whilst the others look on in mute alarm.

'Hello, Carole? It's Matt, is Rosie with you? Have you seen her at all today?'

'Rosie? No, she's not here, Matt. Sorry. Isn't she supposed to be meeting you?'

'Yes, but she hasn't arrived. Is Grace there?'

'I'll just get her for you. You'll have to excuse her, she's been in a complete tizz all afternoon because she's misplaced her phone. Can't find it anywhere. I swear she's surgically attached to that damn thing!'

Matt could hardly contain his panic. The hackles at the back of his neck were rising and he almost snapped at Carole to hurry up, but fortunately Grace took the phone from her mother in seconds.

'Hi Matt. Sorry, I—'

'Grace? Have you seen or heard from Rosie tonight?'

'Not since I saw her in the deli with Dylan earlier this afternoon. Why?'

'I was supposed to meet her here in the Drunken Duck but she hasn't turned up.'

'So where is she?' asked Grace, a wobble in her voice.

'I'm not sure. I've tried calling her but she's not answering her phone. If she's not with you and Abbi, and she's not here with us at the Duck, then she must have gone back home to the café. What I don't understand is why, especially as we have well, a date tonight.'

'I'll call Zara to ask her to go over to the windmill.'

'Zara and Sam have gone to coast with Penny. They won't be there.'

'What about Theo? Did he go with them?'

'No, he stayed behind to work on his tree.'

'Then I'm calling him!'

Grace disconnected the call, but Matt got hold of Theo first and asked him to sprint over to the café to check on Rosie, insisting he remained on the line until he'd found her.

When Theo told him that the windmill was in darkness and there was no reply to his hammering, Matt stomach gave a painful lurch. Did her disappearance have anything to do with their investigation of Theo's accident? Had she become the next victim?

'What are we waiting for? We have to go out and look for her!' declared Freddie, slamming down his pint glass and striding towards the door, his face pale with fear.

'Hang on for a minute, Fred. We need to have a plan first. We should split up and—'

The door burst open and Grace and Josh rushed in, swiftly followed by Abbi, Carole and Roger.

'Matt! What's going on? Where's Rosie? What's happened to her?' asked Reverend Coulson, his voice calm and authoritative, but his forehead displayed parallel lines of worry. 'Who saw her last?'

'I did,' volunteered Dylan. 'When we left Adriano's, she got a text from Grace, told me she'd catch me up, and no one has seen her since.'

'But I couldn't have sent Rosie a text because I've lost my phone. Oh, my God! Someone must have stolen it so they could lure her into a trap!' Grace slumped onto a barstool and promptly burst into tears.

'Matt, I really think we should be—' urged Freddie, hopping from one foot to the other like a toddler desperate to visit the bathroom, anxious to be out doing something, anything.

But Matt was concentrating on cross-examining Grace.

'Where have you been today?'

'At home with Mum and Abbi making up the wedding

favours for Sunday. Surely you're not suggesting that Mum or Abbi...?'

'Did you go out anywhere? Anywhere at all?'

'Just to Adriano's for a coffee.'

'So, someone in the deli could have taken your phone?'

'Well, I suppose?'

'But if Rosie got a text from Grace asking her to meet her, why didn't she turn up at the vicarage?' asked Freddie.

'I have no idea. Okay. Dylan, can you and Abbi go over to the café and help Theo continue the search there? Roger, can you, Carole and Grace search the area around the church and the vicarage? Freddie, Josh and I will do a sweep of the woodland. If Rosie did get a text asking her to meet Grace, then those are the only three places she would have gone without questioning the arrangements. The café, the vicarage, and Ultimate Adventures. Stay in touch!'

Matt sprinted to where he'd left his SUV with Freddie and Josh at his heels. He had never been more terrified in his life. He was now absolutely certain that Rosie's disappearance had something to do with Theo's accident. Clearly the perpetrator thought they were on to them and wanted to put an end to their investigations. He just hoped that this was a stunt to frighten them off, rather than anything more macabre.

They arrived in the car park of the outward-bound centre at such speed that when Matt applied the brakes, a confetti of pebbles flew into the air. As the only light in the compound was from a safety light that had come on automatically, Matt left the headlights trained onto the front door of the reception cabin and jumped from his seat.

All around, the woodland seemed peaceful and serene, the night-time creatures having decided to stalk their prey elsewhere. He was about to dash into the main building to collect the keys to the storeroom when he heard the steady thrum of an engine.

'Do you hear that?'

Matt glanced briefly at Freddie and Josh before racing towards its source. When he reached the door of the storeroom he slowed to a standstill, placing his arm across Freddie's chest to halt his advance. His heart raged, pumping blood around his body so fast he felt faint which only served to increase the sinister thoughts whirling unchecked around his brain.

'Slowly,' he whispered, as they edged around the side of the wooden shed.

Matt peered through the gloom until he was able to distinguish the outline of the stationary quad bike, its engine purring like a contented tiger. In an instant, his eyes followed the route of the incongruous concertinaed tube all the way up to the hole in the wall, its meaning immediately apparent.

'Oh my God!' screamed Matt, lurching forward to yank the hose from the aperture. 'Get inside! Quick!'

When he pulled open the door, the toxic stench of exhaust fumes hit him full in the face and surged down into his lungs. He stretched his fleece over his nose and pushed forward, his brain screaming panic as he fought to open the door to the bathroom.

'Matt! Stand aside!' commanded Freddie, grabbing an evil-looking machete from a hook on the wall. In a single, controlled action, he swung the blade down onto the lock and wrenched the door towards him.

There was Rosie, lying unconscious on the floor.

Matt stooped down and collected her in his arms, her body as limp as a ragdoll's, and rushed outside where he lay her gently on the ground whilst Freddie hurried back into the storeroom for an oxygen tank. As he attached the mask, horror pounded through Matt's veins as he tried to deliver some of his own lifeblood into Rosie's body. Each passing minute seemed to last for hours but he refused to give up.

Oh my God! What if?

A myriad of regrets stormed through his mind, accusing him of being responsible for what had happened to Rosie. Why hadn't they left things to the police? What if she died? With tremendous effort, he banished the blame from his mind. There would be plenty of opportunity for self-indulgent recriminations later.

That first splutter of breath from Rosie's lips was the sweetest poetry Matt had heard in his whole life. It was followed by another, and then another, until Rosie succumbed to a lengthy cacophony of coughing. Matt sat back on his heels and allowed Josh to take over whilst he spent a few seconds cramming his emotions back into their box – now was not the time to fall apart.

'I'll call an ambulance,' said Freddie.

'No. It'll be quicker to take her to hospital in the SUV.'

'You saved Rosie's life, Matt. If you hadn't—'

But Matt wasn't listening. The fact that he'd saved Rosie's life meant very little when it was his fault her life had been in jeopardy in the first place. He settled a silent Rosie on the back seat of his SUV and asked Freddie to take the wheel, whilst Josh called everyone to tell them they'd found Rosie, and then called the police.

'Who do you think did this?' asked Freddie, his eyes focussed on the track ahead as they bucked and bounced towards the main road. A muscle in his cheek worked overtime and he was clearly struggling to control his anger.

'I have an idea but I'm not one hundred per cent sure. I think Rosie and I might have overlooked something, or more precisely, someone.'

'So, you reckon the same person who caused Theo's fall was responsible for this attack on Rosie?'

'Yes. My hunch is that Rosie probably made some throw-away comment about our progress which was overheard. I'm still working my way through an idea that started to niggle when Grace told us her phone had been stolen, but this craziness has to stop now.'

in pondering the tree [illegible] on the back seat of his SUV and asked [illegible] to take the wheel while Josh called everyone to tell them they'd found Rosie and then called the police.

'What do you think caused this?' asked Freddie, his eyes focused on the road ahead as they bucked and bounced towards the main road. A muscle in his cheek worked overtime and he was clearly struggling to control his anger.

'I have an idea but I'm not one hundred per cent sure. I think Rosie and I might have overlooked something, or more precisely someone.'

'So you reckon the same person who caused Olivia's fall was responsible for this attack on Rosie?'

'Yes. My hunch is that Rosie probably made some throwaway comment about our progress which was overheard. I'm still working my way through the ideas that started to niggle when Grace told me her phone had been stolen, but this [illegible] has to stop now.'

Chapter 17

Saturday morning dawned with heavy bulbous clouds and a sharp nip in the air that threatened snow. From her seat on the white leather sofa next to the French windows in the Windmill Café, Rosie surveyed the gathering. The Windmill Café was one of her favourite places in the world and one which she had thought, for a split second in the bathroom at Ultimate Adventures, that she would never see again.

She had been kept in hospital overnight for observation and the doctor had only reluctantly agreed to discharge her that morning on the understanding that she rested and wouldn't engage in anything too strenuous or stressful. She didn't think it wise to mention the deluge of visitors that were expected in the marquee at noon, only two hours away, never mind the preparations for the Willerby wedding of the year and the rehearsal dinner that evening. But she had promised to do as she was told in order to get out of the neon-bright cubicle that was giving her a headache.

Matt looked worse than she did, having spent the night on a row of plastic chairs in the hospital waiting room. She had tried to talk to him on the drive back to the café, about what had happened, about what he had discovered, about the fact that he had saved her life, about their relationship. She wanted him to know that she was staying in Willerby, staying at the café, making her home there for as long as Graham would have her as his chaos-prone manager. She wanted to tell him that she loved him!

However, when she had started mumbling her effusive thanks, Matt had asked her gently to wait until the whole sorry episode had been concluded before they talked about more intimate matters, and she didn't blame him – she thought her head was going to burst with it all.

Someone had tried to kill her!

When she had stepped out of the Ultimate Adventures SUV in the Windmill Café car park, she thought her knees would buckle beneath her. As always, Matt had been there to support her, guiding her past the two police Land Rovers and then upstairs to her circular studio so she could take a shower before making an entrance in the café where everyone was now waiting for Detective Sergeant Kirkham to launch into his explanation of who had been causing havoc in the village.

She'd panicked when Matt had accompanied her down the stairs, his arm around her waist. She realised that her batteries had been severely depleted by the trauma of the events of the previous day and that she wouldn't have the energy to provide their guests with even a cup of tea, never mind the usual surfeit of hospitality the Windmill Café was so famous for.

But she needn't have worried because a battalion of help had descended. Rosie sent a grateful smile in the direction of Mia, the best friend anyone could ever have, standing next to Carole, Grace and Corinne, who was wearing one of Mia's quirky aprons depicting lurid green snowmen. She felt like an invalid aunt as they fussed around her and made sure everyone had been offered a drink.

Her gaze landed on Abbi who was curled up on the opposite sofa, her slender body snuggled in close to Dylan's, her habitual sparkle doused with trepidation as her eyes rested on the policeman and his broad-shouldered colleague stationed at the door. Dylan too emitted an aura of nervousness and, unusually for him, he hadn't touched the croissants Carole had placed on the table in front of him. Freddie however had no such qualms and he loitered next to the police constable stuffing a *pain au chocolat* into his mouth and scattering crumbs on his Ultimate Adventures fleece which he brushed away to the floor. Rosie wasn't surprised that his actions did not ignite her cleaning demons who were too busy sleeping off the effects of her recent turmoil.

She glanced out of the window at the huge over-blown meringue snoozing on the lawn behind the lodges waiting for a gaggle of competitors and their supporters to descend and fill its interior with festive joy and laughter. Despite the tense atmosphere inside the café, she was forced to smile when she saw a group of villagers loitering outside the marquee, eager to use the final two hours to ensure their tree was the best it could be. Once again, Rosie heaved a sigh of relief that she had passed the judging baton on to Reverend Coulson.

'Where's Theo?' she asked.

No sooner had the question exited her lips than she saw Theo appear from inside the marquee, a swagger of confidence in his step as he made his way along the path towards the café. However, he had travelled a mere ten steps when he was intercepted by two uniformed police officers. Even from that distance, Rosie could see his expression change from super-confidence to almost comedic alarm. As she continued to watch, he pointed towards the café, shook his head and made to leave the officers, but they restrained him, attached a pair of handcuffs and led him, complaining vociferously, towards one of the Land Rovers in the car park.

'What's going on?' cried Penny shooting towards the French doors as the police vehicle snaked slowly down the driveway towards the main road. 'Why has Theo been arrested by the police? Does that mean that he, that it was Theo who tried to kill Rosie?'

'Oh my God!' declared Mia and Grace in unison.

'No way!' chorused Dylan and Sam.

'But surely Theo didn't set up the trap in the woods!'

'He must have had an accomplice!'

'Who?'

For the next few minutes, discussion of the new development ricocheted around the café's eaves until it reached screech level and DS Kirkham had to resort to banging his fist on the table to call for order. Whilst his craggy features gave the impression of a kindly teddy bear, his impressive bulk and the steely expression in his pewter eyes brooked no arguments.

'Let me make it clear that Theo Morris has not been detained in connection with the attack on Miss Barnes last night. The reasons for his arrest will become clear in due course. I'm sure you all want to know who's responsible for

Mr Morris's accident as well as what happened to Miss Barnes, so let's get this unpleasant business over with, shall we? Would you all take a seat, please?'

Rosie's had no idea what the detention of Theo meant, or who was about to be frog-marched from the room by DS Kirkham and his colleague. In those long hours laid up in a hospital bed, drifting in and out of sleep because of the constant burble of noise, she had spent her time flicking through her internal Rolodex of theories, trying to produce a spark of inspiration, but her brain felt like a shipment of candy floss had taken up residence. Matt had refused to talk about the investigation on their journey home, and she had respected that.

But was there some clue she had overlooked?

Everything up at Ultimate Adventures had happened so quickly that she hadn't been able to gain any sense of the identity of her assailant beneath the motorcycle leathers and helmet. She didn't even know whether it was a man or a woman.

At first, she had ruminated and cogitated on the possibilities and come to the conclusion that it couldn't have been any of the stag party guests. Sam, Zara and Penny had been at the coast, Theo was busy working on his masterpiece in the marquee, Dylan, she assumed, had been on his way to the Drunken Duck when she'd left him to meet Grace and Abbi at the Ultimate Adventures lodge. On the other hand, none of them had an alibi for the attack on Theo and it had turned out that they all had a pretty strong motive to want him out of their lives.

So who did that leave?

After the assault on *her* life, they could definitely rule out a random stranger as the culprit. It had to be someone connected to the wedding party. She swept the room again for who remained on the list of possible suspects. There was no way she was even going to consider Grace or Josh as possible perpetrators – the thought was just too ridiculous. What bride or groom would have the spare mental capacity to organise and execute something like that? Carole or Gordon? Equally as incongruous! Corinne? Well, she had no connection with Theo and Rosie wasn't even prepared to contemplate the possibility that it could be Mia, Freddie or Matt. Her brain started to hurt from overthinking and the lingering after-effects of the carbon monoxide.

Everyone was now seated and waiting for the DS Kirkham's pronouncements. Sam lounged on a sofa next to Zara, his left ankle crossed casually over his right knee, his right arm draped along the backrest, totally relaxed and unconcerned. It struck her for the first time how extraordinarily good-looking he was with his blond hair teased into a quiff and those startlingly blue eyes crinkling at the corners. She understood how women would be attracted to him when he was away from home on his golfing jaunts, oozing charm and charisma. He was clearly unconcerned that his secret was about to be revealed. Either that or he was in denial.

'As we have Mr Wilson to thank for identifying the person responsible for both Miss Barnes's and Mr Morris's attacks, then I propose to allow him to take the floor. I suggest you listen carefully to what he has to say before asking questions. My constable and I will be watching everyone closely.'

The room fell silent immediately.

'Thank you,' said Matt, before turning to look at Rosie, his expression giving nothing away. 'However, before I start, I want to say that I wouldn't have uncovered any of this without Rosie's help.'

The audience swung their attention from Matt to Rosie and she felt her cheeks glow under their scrutiny. She managed a tentative smile of acknowledgement then averted her eyes, nervously fiddling with the friendship bracelet Mia had given her as an early Christmas present. Spasms of anxiety gnawed at her stomach and tightened her throat. After all, her attacker was somewhere in this room, watching her every move, working out how she had managed to escape with her life, maybe even preparing to lunge for her throat and squeeze and squeeze until her life drained away.

She sought out Carole, who noticed her expression of panic and moved across the room to sit next to her, slotting her palm into hers and giving it a reassuring pat.

'Theo's accident was a shocking thing to happen, even more so because everyone is here to celebrate the forthcoming wedding of two people who are our friends. Grace and Josh were devastated about what happened in the woodland on Wednesday morning and so they asked Rosie and I to put on our metaphorical deerstalkers to see if we could help the police to identify the culprit. We agreed, and when we spoke to each one of you individually, it came as a surprise to discover that Theo seems to have upset you all at some stage *and* that everyone had the opportunity to set up the trip wire that caused him to fall from his cycle.'

A collective intake of breath rolled through the room, but no one uttered a word as they were too busy hanging on Matt's every word.

'One of the things that struck us from the outset was that whoever targeted Theo must have known him extremely well to know he would choose to take that shortcut through the woodland to the finishing line. But then, it's no secret he craves the top prize in everything he puts his mind to, no matter whose toes he has to trample on to get there.'

Relief washed over Rosie that the police had prevented Theo from joining them in the café; it meant that Matt could be as frank as possible about the more unpleasant traits of his personality.

'Josh invited Theo to his wedding because he'd offered to supply the wedding cars. We've heard that his vintage car hire company is a huge success because he's a sharp, savvy businessman, unsentimental about his vehicles' origins, and that he's always on the look-out for a great deal, a tactic that has caused a huge amount of ill-feeling.'

Zara looked up, her dark brown eyes widened, her lips parted, but no words came out. She turned towards Sam, silently pleading for his support. He grabbed her hand and gave it a reassuring squeeze.

'Now look here, Matt. Surely you can't be suggesting that Zara had anything to do with Theo's accident? He's our sons' godfather, for Christ's sake!' Sam blustered with vicarious indignation. 'And if you are also implying that she was responsible for attempting to asphyxiate Rosie up at Ultimate Adventures yesterday, then I suggest you go away and rethink your theory because you are clearly—'

'Please, Mr Vardy, if you would allow Mr Wilson to continue,' snapped DS Kirkham, fixing Sam with a firm glare until he climbed down from his pulpit. 'Thank you.'

'Zara told Rosie and I that Theo had conned her grandfather out of his beloved Rolls Royce, a vehicle that had been his pride and joy and which he had wanted to pass on to the next generation. Sadly, his wish did not come to fruition because of the actions of Theo Morris. He tricked Mr Garstang into signing over the paperwork just weeks before he died. It was a despicable thing to do to an old man and Zara is quite right to have been furious about his deception. However, it does give her a strong motive for wanting Theo to suffer because of how he conducted himself towards a vulnerable member of her family.'

'Motive!' blurted Sam, his eyes bulging with shock. 'Is this some kind of—'

'Mr Vardy,' growled DS Kirkham. 'I shall have to ask you to leave if you're unable to restrict your comments.'

'Sorry.'

Sam sunk back down onto the sofa and this time it was him who gripped Zara's hand for support. Matt waited a couple of beats before continuing with his explanation, his eyes fixed on Sam who refused to look him in the eye.

'It should be noted, however, that Theo *did* pay a reasonable price in the transaction – not the full market value, perhaps, but not so far from it as to raise any suspicions that he'd ripped off the owner – which is the trademark of many a business deal, after all.

'So yes, Zara does have a motive and, like everyone else in the stag party, she had the opportunity to leave her lodge after the men had left for the cycle ride and before the rest of the group woke up and went in search of breakfast. She could have jogged over to the woods, set up the trap and returned without anyone being any the wiser. Okay, it was possible that, for once, Theo might decide to follow the official race route, but what were the chances of that? As we know, Theo Morris doesn't play by the rules.'

'Okay, even if I did have a reason to want Theo to pay for what he did to my family, what about Rosie?' fired Zara, at last galvanised to speak up for herself. 'What possible reason could I have for wanting to hurt her? She's shown us nothing but kindness since we arrived, and if you're going to accuse me of dressing up in leathers and riding one of those quad bikes through the woods by myself before attempting to kill Rosie then you are even crazier than I give you credit for.'

'It does seem a little far-fetched, I agree,' said Matt, pacing across the floor as he considered his next line of attack. 'But everyone knew Rosie and I were asking questions, and unbeknown to her, she said something she didn't realise the importance of, but the perpetrator did. Now that we know the reason Theo was targeted, we know who the culprit is.'

'Who?' demanded Zara.

'All in good time.'

Matt paused in his wandering, his fingers stroking at his clean-shaven chin, and Rosie smiled. He looked exactly how she expected a real detective to look and she wondered, not for the first time, whether he had missed his vocation. She knew that if his father hadn't been involved in the tragic accident that ended his life, Matt would most likely be working in the police service. She watched him meet Zara's eyes and saw her raise her chin and stare back at him with the confidence of a clear conscience.

'But I know it wasn't you, Zara.'

Despite her bravado, Zara closed her eyes briefly and released a long sigh. She relaxed back against Sam, hugging her arms into her chest, and staring at Matt with blatant irritation. But she remained silent, like everyone else, anxious to see in whose direction Matt would launch his next missile.

Chapter 18

Electricity sparkled through the café as Matt's audience anticipated his next pronouncement; every one of them terrified that they would be his next target. Most were contemplating their hands and fingernails as though they were the most fascinating things they had ever seen, yet sent covert glances from beneath their lashes at each other.

'Zara wasn't the only member of the wedding party with cause to loathe Theo, was she Abbi?'

'What do you mean? I didn't loathe him.' Abbi shot back her denial so quickly that it was clear to everyone it was a lie.

'You didn't like him though, did you?'

'Well, you've just told us that a lot of people didn't like him,' Abbi reasoned, her eyebrows raised, her carefully-outlined lips twitching with nerves. 'Why should I be any different?'

'Theo could have made a real nuisance of himself, if he'd wanted to. He could have put a spanner in the works of your fledgling movie career.'

'Abbi? What's Matt talking about?' asked Dylan, his face creasing with confusion.

'When Rosie and I interviewed Abbi, she told us about how worried she was that the director of her current film would discover that she'd lost her licence for drink driving.'

'Is that true, Abbi?'

'Yes, it's true. It's never been a secret, actually. It wasn't my proudest moment and I've moved on. And anyway, if I lose my part in this film there'll be others.'

'I can vouch for Abbi. I know how upset she is about what happened – and it was six years ago!' said Grace, her face as pale as clotted cream.

'Ah, yes, but it wasn't the main reason you were nervous about Theo's threat to stir up trouble, was it?'

'I don't know what you are inferring—' began Abbi, but her expression had morphed from irritation to nervousness.

'I'm referring to the fact that when Theo stumbled across the piece in a local newspaper about your driving conviction, it also reported a more interesting transgression that Theo realised would affect your current career path much more. He was going to reveal your deepest, darkest secret, wasn't he?'

'Abbi? What's he talking about?' asked Dylan, turning in his seat to face her.

'Nothing Dylan—'

'I found the article on the internet yesterday when everyone was busy doing other things.' Matt reached into his pocket and produced a printout which he handed to Abbi. 'This is what Theo showed you on Tuesday night, isn't it? After you'd spent the whole afternoon regaling everyone with details of your starring role in a movie. Did Theo threaten to expose your lapse in integrity when he had an audience, so he could watch you squirm?'

'No.'

'If Theo hated one thing it was being up-staged. So, I think he was waiting to reveal the juicy nugget of information he had stumbled across until the perfect opportunity presented itself, maybe even at the wedding reception. You didn't want your secret to poke its head above the parapet and spoil your future, did you?'

'Abbi, will you tell me what's going on?'

If looks could kill Rosie knew Matt would be gasping for his final breath. Abbi could certainly have landed the part of the Wicked Witch of Willerby in that year's local pantomime without any recourse to her acting skills.

'Do you want to tell everyone, or shall I?'

Any last trace of remaining colour in Abbi's face seeped away and the indignation drained from her body. Her diamanté hairclip and pearl earrings the size of grapes looked brash against her grey complexion.

'Okay. Okay. I am totally ashamed of what I did and I've been trying to put things right ever since. What Theo didn't know, and wouldn't let me explain, was that I've been taking private drama lessons for years. I sat my final exams last month, which I passed with Distinction.'

'What are you talking about?' asked Zara.

'My acting qualifications.' Abbi averted her eyes to concentrate on her manicure, picking at a flake of glitter on her thumbnail as she tried to build up the courage to utter her next few words. 'My sister sat them for me.'

'She did what?' gasped Dylan.

'I'm a twin, you know that. Alicia's much cleverer than I am. She has an almost photographic memory whilst I got stuck with the practicality genes. I was useless at taking exams. I would get so nervous that I would just fall apart. No matter what I tried – and believe me I tried everything – my mind went totally blank every time I sat in front of one of those little desks and was told I could turn over the exam paper. So, I did the practical and Alicia sat the written paper as me. No one guessed, and why would they? She aced it, as I knew she would, and she'd only spent ten days revising the whole two-year syllabus. So I got the grades to get me into drama school.'

'You cheated?'

'Not in my skills as an actor but in putting pen to paper, yes. However, if it's any consolation, I did all the revision alongside Alicia and I could recite every single line of text as well as she could in the comfort of our bedroom. I *am* ashamed of what I did and the guilt has gnawed away at me ever since. It's there every time I go for an audition, every time I start to learn a new piece, every time I rehearse a difficult role, and it's affected my confidence tremendously.

'It came out a year after I'd left college when I was interviewed after an am-dram production of The Sound of Music. A weasel of a reporter splashed his discovery all over the local news. I had to get away so Grace and I went travelling. When I came home, I knew that I had to put in for my exams again. I studied and studied, night after night. It was killing me that I was living as a fraud and I was determined to put things right as far as I could. I took up yoga and even tried hypnosis to help me with my exam nerves, but the thing that saved me was a course of acupuncture. And I did it, passed with flying colours – all by myself.'

Abbi looked around the room, tears rolling silently down her cheeks, but she had recovered some of her rosy complexion. Dylan handed her a serviette which she accepted gratefully and blew her nose.

'And do you know what? Now that I've conquered the shadow of deception, I'm a much better actress, which is probably how I managed to land this movie role. I'd hoped I had atoned for my sins, but when Theo stopped me on Tuesday he had this weird gleam in his eyes. He ordered me to lay off the boasting and handed me a copy of that article. I told him that Grace and her family already knew about it and pleaded with him not to tell everyone else – but he just laughed at me.'

Abbi dried her cheeks and stuffed the tissue up her sleeve before continuing.

'He said he was going to show Dylan the article first as he was the one I had lied to the longest, then he said he was going to read it out as his party piece at the rehearsal dinner tonight. Maximum opportunity for shaming and humiliation, he said. I suppose I deserve it and was prepared to take my punishment. However, he also said he was going to email a copy to the director of my new film. Well, you've heard what sort of person *he* is – I would have been fired on the spot.'

Abbi swallowed down on her distress and the strength of character she had acquired over the years to elbow her way through the battlefield that was the acting profession, returned with a vengeance. She sat up straight, squared her shoulders, and looked directly at Matt.

'You're right. I do dislike Theo, but he's far from perfect himself. He's a manipulative, cold-hearted bully who enjoys belittling people who have the audacity to steal the limelight away from him – even for a few measly seconds. But I had nothing to do with his accident, nor did I follow Rosie into the woods and try to kill her with the exhaust fumes from a quad bike. When you eventually get around to telling us who is responsible for these dreadful things, I will be the first person to...'

'Okay, okay!' Matt held up his palm. 'Don't worry, you're not on our list of suspects!'

Abbi's tears resumed, this time they were tears of relief. In a single movement, Dylan took her into his arms and dropped a kiss onto to top of her head, whispering soothing words into her ear as he stroked the hair from her face.

'For God's sake! Get a move on, Matt, will you? Tell us who did this so we can focus on something else!' said Dylan, a soupçon of annoyance scrawled across his handsome features.

Rosie watched Matt nod, and then swing his eyes in Sam's direction. The bottom dropped from her stomach as she understood what was about to be revealed. She wouldn't want to be in his shoes, but the person she felt most sorry for was Zara. However, what had happened to Theo, and to her, had been a criminal offence and exposing the truth had to be paramount.

Chapter 19

Rosie glanced over at the police constable loitering next to the French windows, then to Freddie and Josh who were blocking the exit door. When her gaze finally came to rest on Sam, he visibly shrunk away from her scrutiny; a shadow of fear stalked across his face as he understood what would happen when Matt revealed his motive for wanting to extract revenge on Theo Morris.

A curl of something akin to sympathy made its way through her chest, not for Sam, but for Zara and their two young sons – too innocent to understand the workings of an adult world, too young to be subjected to the inevitable recriminations, silent or otherwise. There would be no escape from the tension and unspoken accusations as their parents worked their way through the aftermath of the revelation of Sam's affair. She watched Sam swallow several times in quick succession and couldn't fail to recognise the pleading in his eyes.

'Sam? Why is Matt staring at you like that?' asked Zara, her eyes ping-ponging between Sam and Matt, her panic evident. 'Sam?'

'Don't worry, Zara. Sam didn't have anything to do with

Theo's accident, but he certainly entertained the idea of doing something similar.'

Sam remained silent, his jaw clenched, only the flickering of a muscle beneath his eye belying the turmoil rushing through his veins as he braced himself against the grenade that was about to be tossed into his hitherto happy family.

'You asked Theo to be godfather to your children, not because you thought he'd be the best person to guide them through the moral maze but because you thought it would ensure his silence. How could he disclose your secret when he was such an important part of your family?'

'What secret?' demanded Zara. 'Sam, what is Matt talking about? Tell me!'

A spasm of pain jettisoned across Sam's expression and his fingers, still laced through Zara's, trembled. He reached up and ran his right hand through his quiff. Fortunately for Sam he was too choked up to answer his wife's questions immediately.

'Matt?'

'Theo found out that part of a golf course Sam had designed in North Wales had inadvertently been built over the boundary of a nature reserve and had threatened to report the error to the authorities.'

Sam looked up, his lips parted as he met Matt eyes.

'Sam? Is that true?' asked Zara.

Sam remained mute but now for a different reason, but he managed to nod.

'How does Theo know all these things?' exclaimed Zara. 'First Abbi and now Sam!'

'It's a good question, Zara, but before we get into that, perhaps Sam can explain what happened when Theo went to the planning department at the local council to disclose his discovery.'

Sam inhaled a deep breath to steady his swirling anxiety and at last found his voice.

'It's true, Theo did go to the local planners and he was able to produce evidence that the course I'd designed encroached onto protected land. It meant a complete redesign of the layout which incurred extra time and money because they couldn't open the course to the public until it was sorted out. The owners of the golf club were livid and consulted their lawyers who threatened to sue me for loss of revenue and then, as I didn't have the cash to pay the compensation, apply for my bankruptcy.'

'Why didn't I know anything about this?' asked Zara, softly, her eyes filled with compassion.

'I didn't want to worry you. You were pregnant with the twins and—'

'But I could have been there to support you. I could have—'

'I know darling, I know.'

Sam looked at Zara with such adoration, Rosie was relieved Sam had finally understood what he had come so close to losing. She hoped he would now find the strength to be loyal to his family in the future.

'I panicked when I got the letter from the solicitors and the local authority's legal department. When I'd calmed down, I went back over the research I'd done when I drew up the original design. I had office copies of the Land Registry deeds for every parcel of land that formed part of the golf course, and the boundaries were clearly delineated. I laid them out and then compared them with my own finalised plans and I hadn't made a mistake after all. It turned out that the company that managed the nature reserve was the guilty party – *they* had trespassed on the golf club's land, not the other way around. So, they were ordered to amend *their* boundaries, not us. They reimbursed my legal fees and paid for a brand-new fence to delineate the boundary so that no more disputes would arise. They even apologised and the golf club offered me membership for life and an all-expenses trip to The Open that year.'

'And you forgave Theo?' cried Zara.

'He's a complete moron,' announced Penny, shaking her head in disgust.

'I agree! Why did you let him get away with it, Sam?' demanded Dylan, his eyes ablaze.

'Well, you know as well as I do what he's like, Dylan. Best just to move on.'

'Paph!' denounced Zara.

Rosie knew that she and Matt were probably the only people in the room who knew the real reason why Sam had continued to forgive Theo. However, what was taxing her brain was how Theo had collected the snippets of information he'd used to his advantage over those who had thought of him as a friend. How had he become privy to secrets their guardians thought would remain hidden for ever? She was about to find out and it shocked her to the core.

'Mrs Vardy,' said DS Kirkham, stepping forward to relieve

Matt of the explanation baton. 'You want to know how Mr Morris knew the things he did? Well, before I came over here, I made a few enquiries and it just so happens that Theo Morris is an expert in surveillance techniques and intelligence gathering from the time he spent in the Territorial Army. He was asked to leave the TA because it was discovered he'd been keeping meticulous records on his fellow volunteers; personal information, often accompanied by photographs taken without the subject's knowledge or consent, and even documentary evidence he'd printed from the internet. He is, for want of a better word, a snoop.'

'Oh my God!'

'He did what?'

'No way!'

'That's how he found out about all the elderly, or vulnerable-to-persuasion, owners of the vintage cars that he wanted for his collection. He delved into their personal lives until he knew everything there was to know about them, about their families and about their particular foibles. Then, he'd use that knowledge in any way he could to broker a more favourable deal. And his exploitation of people's weaknesses for monetary gain didn't stop at strangers – his surveillance extended to his friends too. You saw him being led away by my officers, and you can rest assured that he'll be questioned about all of these activities just as soon as we've arrested and charged the person who's responsible for attacking him and Miss Barnes.'

Rosie noticed that Dylan's cheeks had reddened when he realised it was his turn to have the spotlight shone into his eyes. She experienced a sharp injection of sympathy for him, and she decided it was time for her to take her turn in the Poirotesque role and explain to the audience that whilst Dylan might have a motive for wanting to harm Theo, there was no way he would have tried to kill *her*.

Chapter 20

'Did you know about what Theo was up to, Dylan?' asked Rosie, replacing the glass of water onto the coffee table in front of her before finding Dylan's eyes, unsurprised to see the pain scrawled across his face. She wished there was a way she could save him from the approaching embarrassment, but there wasn't and the sooner he told his story the quicker they could move on to focus on the real culprit.

'I suspected he was involved in something, but every time I tried to speak to him about it, he deflected my questions – just like he always does. He's always been maddeningly condescending, and his attitude was much worse after I borrowed money from him to save my business and couldn't pay it back. I never made a secret of my financial troubles – Abbi knows I'm in debt up to my ears, she just doesn't know who my banker is.'

'Oh, Dylan—'

'Theo Morris doesn't have a generous bone in his body. He would rather see the young lads I coach joining street gangs than miss an opportunity to teach me a lesson about his superiority and my failures – both as a medic and as a business manager. But I had nothing to do with his accident in the woods. Every ounce of my energy is focused on trying to come up with ways to save the academy. But do you know what? Unlike Sam and Zara who would cheerfully shake hands with whoever did that to Theo, I just want to see them pay for what they've done, especially to Rosie.'

Outside, the earlier flurry of snowflakes had morphed into an insistent squall and the whole scene was now blanketed in a thick coating of white. Rosie saw Reverend Coulson arrive in his ancient Volvo and make his way to the marquee to begin his deliberations. The tension inside the Windmill Café was mounting as the clock ticked towards noon when everyone was expected to be standing next to their Christmas tree waiting for the announcement of the winner of the Christmas Carousel competition.

A murmur of conversation had started to coil around the café as Carole, Mia and Corinne took the opportunity to busy themselves with replenishing the refreshments. Rosie couldn't fail to see the surreptitious glances everyone was sending in Penny's direction. Even Grace seemed to be giving her a wide berth when she handed round a plate of mince pies. But then, Penny *was* the only person that hadn't been mentioned yet, and it was clear everyone thought she was the culprit.

Mia hung her tea towel on the radiator and came to sit with Rosie on the sofa whilst Carole and Corinne stayed in the kitchen, leaning against the work benches with their coffee mugs gripped between their palms. For a fleeting moment, Rosie thought they looked like mother and daughter.

DS Kirkham cleared his throat and a hush descended over the room.

'As you probably know, many violent crimes are committed by someone close to the victim, and this case is no exception.'

Every eye in the Windmill Café switched from DS Kirkham's face to Penny's and her jaw slackened. She remained silent, her mobile phone nestled against her chest as she twisted the silver chains at her neck round and round her fingers. Her kohl-heavy makeup was smudged and gave her a ghoulish appearance.

'After checking Mr Morris's antecedents, we found a number of complaints of harassment and intimidation from former girlfriends. Allegations that he had stalked them, spied on them, questioned them incessantly about their movements, about their choice of friends, about their leisure pursuits. Some complainants understood the control he was exerting over their lives and left before it had an adverse impact on their health; others weren't so lucky and struggled to break free.'

'Penny? Is that true?' asked Zara. 'Did Theo intimidate you?'

Penny didn't reply. She simply sat staring into the distance, stroking the screen of her mobile phone with her thumb, her eyes glazed, her face serene, as if she'd escaped into a different world.

'Penny?'

No response.

'Penny?' Carole went to sit on the bar stool next to Penny, placing her arm around the girl's shoulders. 'Penny? Is what DS Kirkham just told us true?'

Penny nodded. A few seconds later, she seemed to emerge from her fugue and recover her power of speech.

'Yes, it's true. Theo always asks where I'm going, who I'm meeting, how long I'm going to be and when I'll be home. I mean precisely when I'll be home – to the minute! He texts me all the time, too. At first, I thought it was sweet, that he was doing these things because he cared about me, that he wanted me to be safe, or that he wanted to spend as much time as possible with me. We've only been together for a few months, but it became claustrophobic. I did try to talk to him about it, to assure him he had nothing to worry about, but nothing changed.'

'Did you know about his surveillance of other people?' asked Rosie.

'God, no! What surprised me was that despite being so obsessed with what I was doing, he still talked about his ex all the time. If he was so keen to know where I was, why did he disappear for hours on end without any explanation? When I asked him about it, he had no qualms in telling me that he was meeting her for coffee. I couldn't understand it. He refused to tell me her name or anything about her. All I knew was that she lived near Birmingham. Oh, and that she'd taken their dog with her when they'd split up and he was simply checking on its welfare. I think if he could have got an order from the court to have access to the dog then he would have done.'

'And you were planning to end your relationship with Theo after Grace and Josh's wedding?'

'Yes, in fact I was so upset after he had a go at me about

the photographs I'd taken on Tuesday that I actually thought of going home straight away. If Grace hadn't asked me to do her a sketch of St Andrew's as a wedding present then I would have packed my bags and disappeared. No wonder his ex-girlfriend left him, though why she still agreed to meet up with him for "coffee" is anyone's guess. I never want to see Theo again.'

'And now you won't have to.'

Penny glanced at DS Kirkham. 'I didn't have anything to do with his accident. Why would I? He hadn't had time to grind me down. And before you ask, I had nothing to do with the attack on Rosie either.' She looked across to the sofa where Rosie was watching her closely. 'I would never do anything like that, you have to believe me!'

Rosie smiled. Call it instinct, call it intuition, she was just sure that Penny didn't have it in her to carry out such an evil deed. But if Penny hadn't installed the tripwire, then who had? She scanned the room again. The only people remaining were Carole, Grace and Josh – a ridiculous suggestion – and Mia, Freddie and Corinne – equally as nonsensical. She couldn't maintain her counsel any longer.

'So, are you going to arrest someone or not?' she blurted.

'I am, Miss Barnes. But before I do, perhaps I can ask Miss Grant to hand me her phone.'

DS Kirkham strode across to the bar stool where Penny was sitting and held out his hand. She scrunched up her nose in confusion but held out her mobile. Everyone held their breath as they watched the police officer flick through the images.

'Whilst I'm satisfied that you had nothing to do with Theo's accident, Miss Grant, it was something *you* did that led the perpetrator to act. They had no choice, in fact.'

'What do you mean?' Penny's voice carried a tremor of uncertainty. 'I didn't do anything!'

'Did you take this photograph?'

'Yes, I took all the photographs on my phone, but I—'

'You see, it was this image that set Theo on the path to his fate. It's why he made such a fuss when you showed him it to him. And why he interrogated you so harshly to find out where the photograph had been taken and when.'

'But it's a picture of a dog!'

'Yes, it is.'

Penny cast her eyes over to Carole. 'It's Alfie.'

'What?' Carole and Grace cried in unison.

Grace leapt from her seat next to Rosie to peer at the camera screen, then she relaxed. 'Oh, no, that's not Alfie. That's Coco, Corinne's dog.'

Every eye in the room swung over to where Corinne was leaning against the kitchen worktop. She seemed to wither before their eyes. Rosie's heart gave a surprise thump against her ribcage before bouncing down into her stomach and ricocheting into her throat as the final piece of the jigsaw puzzle slotted into place. The image wasn't crystal clear yet but it was beginning to come into focus.

'Why was Theo so interested in a photograph of Corinne's dog?' asked Carole, returning to her position next to Corinne to offer her some moral support.

'Because,' said DS Kirkham, 'correct me if I'm wrong, Miss

Shaw, Coco belonged to Mr Morris, too. You were his girlfriend before Penny, weren't you?'

An uncomfortable silence expanded into every corner of the room as everyone tried to process this unexpected piece of information.

'*You're* his ex?' spluttered Penny, staring at the shell-shocked Corinne.

The police constable at the French windows adjusted his position, Freddie and Josh did likewise so that all exits were covered should Corinne decided to bolt. But they needn't have worried. Corinne wasn't going anywhere. She just stood, slumped against Carole like a puppet clipped of its strings, defeated and dejected.

'Yes. I am.'

'But how? Why? Did Theo—'

'Perhaps you'd like to explain your reasons for what you did?' offered DS Kirkham.

Corinne glanced around the room until her eyes came to rest on Grace whose face was a melange of shock, confusion and disbelief.

'I'm so sorry, Grace. I really am. The last thing I wanted to do was spoil your wedding. I'm really grateful for your friendship, for helping me to believe that I could start over again after escaping from the torture that Theo subjected me to. I really thought I'd managed to leave my past behind and that I could look forward to a happier future. You and Carole and Roger have been so kind to me – you don't deserve any of this. I'll never forget how you accepted me and made me feel part of the community. I'm so, so very sorry...'

'But I don't understand,' began Grace, bewildered by what Corinne was saying. She dragged her eyes from Corinne to look questioningly across at Matt and Rosie. 'Why?'

Corinne had depleted her reserves of courage and burst into tears, hiding her face in Carole's chest who stroked her hair and muttered soothing sounds. Corinne's whole body juddered and shook as the magnitude of what she'd done and its consequences reverberated around her audience. Everyone was struggling to understand what was going on, and the noise level continued to climb until DS Kirkham cleared his throat and said 'Perhaps I can explain?'

The heated conversation abated and silence fell, save for Corinne's weeping.

'You heard Miss Grant tell us that she thought Mr Morris had an unhealthy fixation with his ex-girlfriend; that he regularly disappeared to meet up with her for coffee. Well, I suspect that it wasn't an innocent coffee and he wasn't *meeting* Miss Shaw but he was using the time to search for her – to follow up on any lead that might give him a clue as to her whereabouts. I've said I think his behaviour bordered on compulsive, but it was worse than that. He was an extremely focussed and obsessive individual who was furious that his girlfriend had managed to escape from him.

'Our records show that a year ago, Miss Shaw made a complaint to the police about Mr Morris's treatment of her. She gave a statement detailing the regime of emotional abuse he subjected her to until she felt her freedom to be herself had been severely eroded. But, as happens so often in these matters, Mr Morris talked her round and there was no prosecution. He probably promised to mend his ways so she agreed to give him another chance. However, I suspect things didn't go as she expected and eventually she found the courage to leave.'

DS Kirkham paused. Everyone's attention was focused on him. Even Corinne had stopped sobbing, her eyes wide with fear as she waited for him to continue.

'It seems Miss Shaw found her way here to Norfolk and thought she was safe at last. She relaxed and started to enjoy her new life. But, in a cruel twist of fate, Miss Grant showed Mr Morris a photograph of a caramel-haired Lhasa Apso whom he recognised immediately. He had to make sure it was definitely Coco so—'

'I saw him through the deli window,' said Corinne, her voice wobbling as she took up the story. 'At first, I couldn't believe it was Theo, but it was and I was absolutely terrified that he'd found out where I was. I knew he was going to do something terrible to punish me for running away. I realised what I had to do if I didn't want to go back to my old life.'

Corinne inhaled a long, ragged breath before continuing.

'I honestly can't remember exactly what happened. The details are all a bit of a blur, like I was sleepwalking or something. But yes, it was me who set up the tripwire. It wasn't that difficult. I knew about the cycle ride, and I walked Coco in the woods every day so I knew about the shortcut. I suspected Theo would have surveyed the route for any chance of beating the competition. So, I just took Coco for her usual early morning walk and twisted the wire between the two trees. I wasn't really expecting it to work, to be honest, but I wasn't thinking straight. I knew there was no guarantee he'd take that shortcut through the woods. When I got home, I just crawled under my duvet and waited – either for Theo to come and get me or for him to meet his fate. I didn't have the energy to run away again.'

Corinne's voice tailed off, tears rolling silently down her cheeks again as she stared beseechingly at Carole.

'I'm so sorry, Carole. I don't know what came over me but I'd put up with Theo's controlling behaviour for too long. He'd chipped away at my self-esteem so much that I couldn't even think for myself any more. I had no confidence in my ability to stand up to him. He ruled every aspect of my life; from what I ate and wore, to who I met and what I did and I realised I was powerless to do anything about it. I knew he followed me everywhere I went, photographed me and recorded details of my every move in his journals. I'd just dug myself into a hole of self-denial and given up.

'Then, one day he came home with Coco and I fell in love with her. She was my saviour. She returned every ounce of my affection and I adored her. Of course, Theo had banked on that happening and Coco became another weapon to threaten me with. If I didn't agree to go with him to inspect another one of his old bangers, he threatened to poison Coco. Or if I refused to put on a show of domestic bliss when we met his parents, then he would make sure Coco would suffer the consequences. I couldn't let him do that so I just went along with everything he wanted.'

'What a monster!' spluttered Mia, her eyes wide with horror.

'I was amazed when he agreed to let me take Coco to the

local park for her walks until I realised why. He used to follow me with his camera to record every move I made. But I loved being outside with Coco so I shoved the image of him lurking in the bushes, watching me, stalking me, into the back of my mind and got on with enjoying the bond Coco and I had built, and the exercise did us both good. I met other dog walkers and we exchanged a few smiles which kept me going. Next it was the odd hello and snippets about our dogs' quirks and characters. I began to feel better, to glimpse a little of my old self beneath the fog of despair and I started to plan my escape.'

Corinne paused and Carole poured her a glass of water which she accepted gratefully.

'Then, Theo told me he'd arranged to view a vintage Rolls Royce that he was very excited about. He told me what a great deal it was and that he couldn't miss the opportunity to snatch it before anyone else did. I think it must have been your grandad's car, Zara. I knew this was my chance to put my plan into action. I faked a sickness bug, even spent an unpleasant hour locked in the bathroom retching so he would have to leave without me or risk losing his "great deal".

'I'd also done my research. It was an hour's drive to where the owner lived and the same back again. I sent up a prayer to the gods of traffic management that there would be a hold-up somewhere on the route. I slung a few bits and pieces into a suitcase – just my passport, driver's licence, that sort of stuff – grabbed some of Coco's things and left. I had nowhere to go but I decided that even living on the streets was better than living with Theo.'

Rosie had never known the café to be so quiet as Corinne's audience was entranced by her story.

'I took a train to Norwich and met up with a woman from Women's Aid who adored Coco and gave me the details of a hostel that welcomed people with dogs. That was a turning point – once again I have Coco to thank for saving me from sleeping in a shop doorway. The lady who ran the hostel fell in love with her as well, and it was Olga who saw the Help Wanted sign in Adriano's Deli when she was in Willerby for a weekend break. It was the perfect solution and, unless I was exceptionally unlucky, Theo would never find me there. I thought life couldn't get any better. I could pay all my bills and keep Coco in dog chews, and when I met Carole and Alfie I knew I had found a place I could call home.'

Corinne glanced up at Carole and gave her a weak smile as tears continued to slip soundlessly down her cheeks.

'As it turned out, my guardian angel had gone AWOL again. When I saw Theo peering in the window of the café, I thought I was hallucinating. Obviously, I know now that Penny's photo of Coco had led him to the village, but at the time and I thought he'd tracked me down. I was terrified and I knew exactly what he would do; target Coco. Everything I did from that moment until I woke up on Wednesday lunchtime is like a distant dream – something that happened to someone else, an episode of wishful-thinking. The reality of what I'd done only really hit me later when I heard he was in hospital. I... I'm sorry oh, I'm so sorry'

Corinne crumbled. She began to rock forwards and backwards, her face buried in her hands, a strange keening noise emanating from deep within her body, like an injured animal caught in a trap. The sound sent shivers down Rosie's spine as she tried to decipher her feelings about what Corinne was confessing.

'But what about Rosie?' demanded Mia, staring at Corinne, her mouth slightly ajar with incredulity. 'What did she ever do to you? You tried to kill her!'

Corinne shook her head. 'No, no, no, I'm so sorry… I don't know… I just…'

'You just what?' Mia had no intention of letting Corinne off without an explanation.

'I'm sorry, Rosie, but when I overheard you talking to Dylan and the girls in the deli I realised that it was only a matter of time before you or Matt discovered the truth. I knew you'd keep digging until you found out about me and Theo. I just went into autopilot, I suppose. I stole Grace's phone from her bag and when Rosie and Dylan left, I sprinted over to Ultimate Adventures, broke into the storeroom and stole one of the quad bikes. I sent Rosie a text from Grace's phone asking her to meet me. I only really wanted to frighten you, Rosie.'

This time, Corinne completely broke down, her distress agonising for everyone to hear. Carole gathered her into her arms, but no one else moved as they continued to process Corinne's extraordinary story and slotted her revelations into their personal puzzle of the events that had taken place over the last four days. DS Kirkham nodded to his constable who removed a pair of handcuffs, and, supported by Carole, Corinne was escorted mutely from the café without complaint.

'I'm going with Corinne!' announced Penny, slipping down

from the bar stool and striding off in their wake. 'The police need to know that everything Corinne has told us about Theo is true. I'm going to make a statement about my own experiences and even if it only helps in a small way, it'll be worth it. What Theo did to her was outrageous!'

As the remainder of the group watched from the French windows, Corinne was assisted into the back of the police Land Rover with Carole on one side and Penny on the other. Silence spread through the Windmill Café. There was no gasp of relief that Theo's attacker had been arrested, no triumph that it was all over and things could get back to normal, just a blanket of sadness for the distress that had been caused.

'Rosie?' whispered Mia. 'Are you okay?'

She met her friend's eyes and nodded, unable to formulate the words to describe the cauldron of emotions that churned through her body. She had expected to feel anger, fury even, when the identity of her assailant was revealed, but Corinne's prolonged emotional abuse at the hands of Theo tugged at her heartstrings and she was filled with sympathy for what she had been through and how it had ushered her towards the edge of her sanity.

She hoped that Corinne would be treated with understanding by the judicial system, and that the role Theo had played in his own suffering would be taken into account, not to mention his use of illegal surveillance techniques. For her own part, she would work on forgiving Corinne because it was clear to everyone with an ounce of empathy that she hadn't been in full possession of her senses.

Chapter 21

'Wow! Isn't it pretty?' cried Mia as she cantered through the snow, bending down to collect an armful of the fluffy white stuff to toss in Freddie's direction as they all made their way towards the marquee whose door had been flung open to welcome the competitors and the guests inside after the judging had been completed.

Mia was right, the scene was Christmas card perfect. From the sails of the windmill, to the eaves of the wooden lodges and the shepherd's hut, to the gable of the marquee, everything had been dusted with a generous sprinkle of snow that glistened under the weak midday sunshine.

'Hey!' squealed Grace as a huge snowball landed on the top of her head. She spun round to see Josh sprinting away, his heels kicking up confetti-like flakes as he tried to make a swift getaway.

But Grace was having none of it. She chased after him and, as everyone watched on in amusement, she managed to catch him and deposit a handful of snow down the back of his neck. In turn, Josh grappled with his wife-to-be, pulled her down into the snow where they made a duo of snow angles whilst giggling uncontrollably. The ensuing laughter from their appreciative audience was exactly the tonic everyone needed to release the pent-up tension of the morning and lighten the mood.

'Want to join in?' asked Matt, raising his eyebrows in Rosie's direction.

'No way!' She shot back before she even thought about it.

However, Matt wasn't going to take no for an answer. He grabbed Rosie around the waist, twirled her into his arms and together they dropped to the ground next to Grace and Josh. Holding her hand tightly, Matt guided them into creating their own snow-angle couple. Rosie's reticence melted and she joined in, copying Grace as she jumped up and launched into a virgin patch of snow to carve out another celestial imprint.

'Yay!' shouted Mia dragging Freddie into the melee until everyone was rolling around in the snow, laughing, giggling, shrieking their objections, singing snatches from Disney tunes until the whole field looked like a battle zone.

'God, I needed that!' sighed Matt, his lips inches from Rosie's ear, his warm breath sending shivers of desire through her veins as he dragged her upright and ushered her towards the warmth of the marquee.

'Me too. I suddenly feel as though a huge block of concrete has been lifted from my chest and I can breathe freely again. Thanks Matt. Thanks for everything. For continuing to dig for information until you found out the truth about Theo, for uncovering his treatment of Corinne, for rescuing me from the storeroom at Ultimate Adventures, but most of all for...'

Rosie found she had a lump the size of a boulder lodged in her throat as a deluge of emotions ambushed her once again. However, she didn't want to wait a minute longer before telling Matt how she felt about him. When everyone had disappeared into the tent, expelling gasps of delight at the festive spectacle, she turned to face him, delving into his eyes, and loving what she saw reflected in their depths. She adored the way her whole body zinged with pleasure whenever he was by her side and she realised how lucky she was to have found someone who instilled such emotions in her.

'I'm sorry we didn't get to have dinner together last night because there was something I wanted to tell you.'

'Me too, but you first.'

'I'm staying here in Willerby, Matt. The windmill is my home; I love the village, the café, the visitors who stay at the lodges, but most of all I love the fact that I'm part of a close-knit community who look out for each other, offer their love and support where it's needed without question or expectation. But you know what the best part of coming to Willerby has been?'

'What?'

'Meeting you. You've helped me realise that home is not about bricks and mortar, a comfortable place to lay your head and amass material possessions. It's about the relationships you form with the people around you, about giving back, spending those coins of happiness and reaping the rewards. When I arrived at the café I was sad, miserable, heart-broken and you made me stop and put things into perspective, challenged me to step outside my comfort zone and try things I would never have dreamed possible. If I'd told Georgina I'd taken part in an assault course she would be straight on the phone to a therapist! I mean, it involved mud, and lots of it! I know I have some way to go before I eradicate my obsession with hygiene, but I'm optimistic. And I have you, Matt, to thank for all this.'

Rosie thought Matt was about to say something, but he decided to show her instead. After holding her eyes for a moment that seemed to last an eternity, he bent forward and his lips met hers, warm, soft, delicious and she kissed him back until she was breathless.

Her whole body suffused with a feeling of home-coming, of being exactly where she was meant to be, wrapped in Matt's arms, sheltered from the world. She would have happily stayed under the eaves of the huge white marquee for the rest of the day if Reverend Coulson hadn't sent out a search party to find them.

'Hey, lovebirds! They're about to announce the winners,' declared Freddie, his freckled face split into a wide smirk. 'Come on, there'll be plenty of time for all this canoodling later!'

Rosie laughed, linked her arm through Matt's and followed Freddie inside, relishing the blast of crushed pine needles coupled with a heavy base note of warm Christmas spices coming from the makeshift bar in the corner. The place was packed with people milling around the trees, chatting animatedly about their favourite design, laughter ricocheting around the canvas walls, the occasional camera flash flickering through the throng. Christmas carols tinkled from a radio in the background and children ducked and dived into the roped off areas causing their parents much consternation.

Rosie caught a glimpse of Dan Forrester, Willerby Gazette's intrepid reporter, who made bee-line for them as soon as he spotted them. Thankfully, Freddie stepped into his path and piloted him away before he could engage Rosie or Matt in a long session of in-depth analysis of the most recent tribulations to befall the Windmill Café.

'Want to take a quick tour of the entries before the winner is announced?' asked Matt, his arm draped over Rosie's shoulder, a gesture that infused her with a golden glow of belonging.

'Absolutely! They all look amazing – I'm so glad I passed the judging baton on to the Rev! Shall we start with Penny's and make our way round the circle towards Theo's?'

'Actually, Theo's been disqualified,' said Mia, joining them on their inspection circuit, a glint of satisfaction in her eyes as she handed them both a glass of warm mulled wine to thaw out their frozen fingers. 'His entry was inspired, though, I'll give him that. The theme he chose was vintage toy cars, trains, vans, cycles, scooters, all hung from the branches by tiny silver chains. Must have taken him ages to source everything from the internet, and he must have spent a fortune too.'

'Wow! Penny is just so talented, isn't she?' sighed Rosie as she feasted her eyes on Penny's finished tree, bestowed with a cornucopia of hand-painted woodland animals scampering through its branches.

'It is gorgeous,' mused Mia, considering Penny's artistry as though it was a Cézanne. 'But if I had to choose my favourite, it would be Abbi's. I would die for one of her hand-made handbags, even a miniature one – especially that white one embroidered with holly berries. Do you think she'll consider selling a few of the decorations to the needy when the competition is over?'

Rosie laughed at the way Mia was drooling over Abbi's competition entry. It was an absolute riot of colour, easiest the brightest one in the room. The kaleidoscope of colours zinged against the verdant backdrop of the dark green foliage, and there was even a full-sized handbag-wallet-keyring combo hiding the ugly brass stand.

'Oh my God!' gasped Rosie, coming to an abrupt standstill when she arrived at the next tree, her palm flying her mouth. 'Mia, you are a genius! Thank you, thank you, thank you, for stepping into the breach – this is absolutely amazing.'

Rosie reached out to Mia and enveloped her friend into a tight hug of appreciation. Whilst she had been distracted with the investigation into Theo's accident, Mia had been quietly holding the fort, not only at the café making sure all the food and drink was ready for the celebration, but she had even carved out some time to finish decorating the Windmill Café's contribution to the Christmas Carousel competition.

Whilst all the entries were identified by a number to ensure anonymity, it wouldn't take the winner of Mastermind to work out who each tree belonged to – and Mia and Rosie's tree was no exception. Dangling from every branch was a tiny silver kitchen implement, from whisks, spatulas, cheese graters and slotted spoons, to egg slicers, corkscrews and even a marshmallow toasting folk. It was stunning, especially to the eyes of the culinary-obsessed Rosie who scrutinised every branch, oohing and ahhing at each new discovery.

'Okay, ladies and gentlemen!' announced the gravelly tones of Reverend Coulson, his voice reverberating through the tent and encouraging the guests and competitors to gather around the makeshift rostrum that had been cobbled together for him from a couple of beer crates. 'A very warm welcome to the inaugural Windmill Café Christmas Carousel competition. First of all, as you probably all know, the unpleasantness that has been lingering over our village this week is over and I hope we can quickly put the drama behind us and move on.'

Rosie giggled when she saw the stern look Roger Coulson bestowed upon Dan Forrester over his half-moon glasses. At least the reporter had the grace to blush and offer the Reverend a reluctant nod.

'Now, when Rosie and Mia asked me to step into the role of judge for this competition I had no idea how difficult it would be to choose a winner. I think you will all agree with me that every tree is a work of festive art and I think the architects of such sparkling magnificence should be given a round of applause.'

A clatter of clapping rolled through the room, accompanied by whistles and the stamping of feet. Rosie took a moment to glance around the gathering. In the absence of Carole, Grace and Josh stood next to Rev Coulson performing the role of bodyguard should the results not go the way some people hoped and they decided to bend the vicar's ear. Both looked relaxed and happy, at last able to enjoy every minute of the lead-up to their wedding celebrations. Next to them was Freddie, his arm around Mia, happiness exuding from every pore as he leaned forward to drop a kiss on her lips.

Rosie picked out Sam and Zara and laughed when she saw that Zara was wearing a pair of clog baubles as earrings and had fashioned a long necklace from a length of brown string and one of her wooden windmills that had been painted in their signature peppermint and white colours. Abbi and Dylan stood behind them, hanging on the vicar's every word as they waited for him to utter those immortal words.

'And the winner is...'

Complete silence descended on the tent, save for the jingle of sleigh bells that Archie had hung above the entrance alongside a huge bunch of mistletoe that swayed in the breeze.

'Tree number eight! Congratulations!'

Rev Coulson grabbed the silver trophy in the shape of a windmill and waited for the winner to rush up, grab it from him, and gush out a speech of effusive thanks, but no one arrived.

'Whose is number eight?' asked Rosie, peering over her shoulder at the carousel until her eyes came to rest on the tree in question. She hadn't had chance to scrutinise the winning tree in detail, but she could see why the Rev had chosen it as the winner. It had none of the perfectly sculpted ornaments, nor the symmetrical aesthetics of the other entries. In fact, a first glance, it was haphazard collection of random objects. However, on closer inspection, there was a definite theme – sports equipment.

There were mini footballs, rugby balls, cricket balls, golf

balls, and tennis balls; rackets, bats and paddles, tiny longbows and quivers filled with arrows, hockey sticks, fishing rods, even a tiny lacrosse stick. The winter sports hadn't been forgotten either; there were miniature skis, taboggans, sledges, snowboards, and what Rosie suspected were curling stones. The variety of sports represented was vast and the tree could belong to only one pair.

'Oh my God! Matt, it's yours! Yours and Freddie's!'

'What?'

'You've won!'

Rosie pogoed up and down on the spot, her excitement swirling through every cell in her body. She flung her arms around Matt's neck and kissed him, laughing when she saw the look of incredulity on his handsome face. Next to her, Mia was doing exactly the same with a stunned Freddie until the audience urged the two men forward to accept the trophy and pose for the obligatory photographs so that the eating and drinking could start.

'Three cheers for our worthy winners!'

The crowd dutifully chorused their congratulations before stampeding towards the tables that were groaning with festive fayre with almost indecent haste. Rosie hung back, letting Mia and Grace man the tables to ensure order reigned and the whole party didn't descend into a bunfight.

After all, they'd had enough accidents in the last six months at the little Windmill Café to last a lifetime.

Epilogue

'Come on! Come on! Grace is getting ready to throw her bouquet!' cried Mia, dragging Rosie into the middle of a coterie of excited women waiting on the steps of the village hall, their breath spiralling into the cold afternoon air.

The meteorological gods had answered Grace's prayers and overnight had delivered an extra layer of powder-soft snow to endow the village of Willerby with a fairy tale aura for her wedding day. The ceremony, conducted by a very proud Reverend Coulson, had been an emotional affair, particularly when he had spoken movingly of his daughter Harriet, referring to her as an angel watching the proceedings from her perch in the clouds.

'Ready?' called Grace, beaming widely, looking every inch the perfect bride in her ivory wedding gown that sparkled with a cascade of crystals. To keep off the chill, she wore a matching velvet shrug edged in faux fur and fastened with a diamante broach that had belonged to her grandmother. She held up the bouquet that Rosie had lavished such love on creating and waved it at the crowd who were waiting like coiled springs in front of her.

'Yes!' they chorused.

'Got a strategy?' whispered Mia as she jostled her way the centre stage.

Rosie giggled. 'Do I need one?'

'Well, have you seen the competition? I calculate the odds as seven to one. Not bad, but with a bit of preparation, I reckon they could be lowered to four to one.'

'How?'

Rosie assessed their fellow contenders. There was Zara, but as she was already married Rosie knew she wouldn't be elbowing anyone aside to snatch the prize. The previous evening, Sam had confided in Matt that he and Zara had decided to take the plunge and relocate with the boys to Florida where his next golf course commission was taking him. Sam had thanked them for their discretion and had assured them he had learnt his lesson and from now on his family would come first. Their move to the US was intended as a fresh start and he was well aware of how lucky he was.

She shifted her surveillance to where Abbi had staked out her place, shoulder-to-shoulder with Mia, in the middle of the circle of women. She smiled and glanced towards the door of the village hall where Dylan loitered with Matt and Freddie, a pint of beer in his hand, watching the event unfold with interest. If his grin was any wider, thought Rosie, his cheeks would split. But she was happy for him. That morning, Christmas Eve, he had received a call he had never expected to happen. A former academy student had signed a lucrative contract with a Championship football team and wanted to show his appreciation to the man who had made his dream come true by offering to sponsor the club for the next two seasons.

Rosie caught sight of Penny, loitering on the periphery of the gathering, her camera raised as she attempted to catch the perfect action shot. Penny's passion for her chosen profession shone from every pose she directed, and she had been overjoyed when she'd received not only compliments but requests for consultations for summer weddings. Rosie hoped that Penny would be able to put what had happened with Theo behind her and move on, just as she herself had after Harry. However, Rosie knew that Penny would be making no attempt to join in the scrum.

As the remaining women in the group were either married or Carole's friends from the WI, it occurred to Rosie that meant Mia was including her in the mix. She knew it was only a bit of fun, but did she really want to catch the bridal bouquet as much as Mia and Abbi did? A shiver of pleasure ran the length of her spine as she caught Matt's eye and saw him smile at her, raising his eyebrows suggestively.

'Woof!' cried Alfie, rushing over to Mia and bouncing on the spot just like his friend was doing.

'Okay! One, two, threeee...'

Grace spun round and threw her bouquet over her shoulder. A very undignified scramble ensued as, in unison, the female guests leapt into the air, their hands outstretched as they reached for the flowers. Rosie felt a sharp shove to her ribs which caused her to stumble to her left, followed by a loud squeal of delight. Abbi had managed to grab the posy and was hugging it protectively to her chest for fear it would be wrenched from her arms.

As Rosie watched, she saw Dylan pass his glass to Freddie – whose face was scrawled with amusement and not a little relief – and stride purposely towards Abbi. As the crowd burgeoned to include the whole wedding party keen to watch the unfolding drama, Dylan came to a stop in front of his girlfriend, took her hands in his and held her eyes. Rosie realised what was about to happen before Abbi did as Dylan lowered himself onto one knee.

'Abbi Jayne Spencer. You are the best thing that has ever happened to me. I love you more than anything in the world. Will you marry me?'

'Yes! Yes! Yes!'

Abbi unceremoniously shoved the bouquet into Rosie's hands and threw herself into Dylan's arms to the delight of the wedding party who applauded the newly engaged couple with enthusiastic whoops and shrieking whistles.

'Never mind, Rosie. It'll be your turn one day,' smirked Matt who had appeared at her side, nodding towards the third-hand bouquet she was clutching in her hands.

Rosie stared into his chocolate-brown eyes and a spasm of desire shot through her chest. Her thoughts drifted back to that morning when she had stood next to him whilst they watched Grace and Josh exchange their vows at the altar of St Andrew's Parish Church. She had turned to offer him a smile of gratitude for being the best friend a girl could wish for and the intensity of his expression had made her gasp.

Dressed in his morning suit Matt was heart-stoppingly

gorgeous. But the bond that had developed between them over the last six months was based on much more than a purely physical attraction. Despite resolving to leave the hearts-and-flowers stuff to Mia after what had happened with Harry, Matt had shown her how to live and love again. He'd encouraged her not only to step outside of her comfort zone but to march away from it with her head held high and with no backward glances.

Okay, so she might fall flat on her face, but so what? All she had to do was pick herself up, brush herself down and start again. And whilst she dearly hoped that there would be no further incidents at the Windmill Café that required them to dust off their metaphorical deerstalkers, she knew that whatever happened, with the support of Matt, Mia and Freddie, she would cope. Not just cope, flourish! With friends like them walking by her side, through the good times and the bad, she was truly blessed.

She reached up to kiss Matt's cheek.

'What's that for?'

'For being you.'

Matt's lips curled into that familiar, mischievous smile causing dimples to appear in his cheeks as he delved deep into her eyes. A helix of electricity coiled through Rosie's veins as Matt closed the gap between them, the fragrance of his citrusy cologne tickling her nose and caused her spirits to soar.

'Happy?'

'Absolutely,' Rosie muttered, not wanting to break the magic of the moment.

As the thrum of the music changed from a rendition of White Christmas to the Mariah Carey classic Rosie loved, it was the perfect moment for her surrender to Matt's kiss. She couldn't have asked for a better Christmas gift and it was a fitting end to the best day of her life.

Acknowledgements

My thanks, as always, to my fabulous editor, Charlotte Ledger, who has the amazing ability to add extra sparkle to my stories. Thanks to my family for listening to me bounce ideas around for the hundredth time without glazing over with boredom, and for taste-testing the Windmill Cafe's Christmas recipes in the middle of June! And a 'high five' to my friend Carol whose namesake became the vicar's wife in this story, along with her faithful, beloved Lhasa Apso, Alfie.

HELP US SHARE THE LOVE!

If you love this wonderful book as much as we do then please share your reviews online.

Leaving reviews makes a huge difference and helps our books reach even more readers.

So get reviewing and sharing, we want to hear what you think!

Love, HarperImpulse x

Please leave your reviews online!

amazon.co.uk kobo goodreads Lovereading iBooks

And on social!

/HarperImpulse @harperimpulse

@HarperImpulse